Dinosaurs, Dilemmas & Albert Einswine

Dino Magic

Book 2

Cover artwork by Sanja Gombar

www.bookcoverforyou.com

Interior artwork by Cauldron Press

www.cauldronpress.ca

A huge thank you to-

Allison Woerner for Alpha Reading.

Maxine Meyer for Copy Editing.

Imogen Evans for Proofreading & Editing.

DINO MAGIC
BOOK TWO

DINOSAURS, DILEMMAS
& Albert Einswine

SEDONA ASHE

CONTENTS

This is a spicy read with detailed intimate scenes.

Look away now if sexy dino shifter men with special 'equipment' isn't your thing!

This book is not based on science, and I enjoy playing with the ideas of what we might have gotten wrong. It is meant to be a book to keep you laughing, not teach you about dinosaurs and real science stuff.

Also, keep in mind I may have stretched the truth about dinosaurs being able to shift into sexy men.

Three dinosaurs stumble across a magic lamp.
When they rub it, a genie appears in a cloud of golden smoke.
"I have three wishes, so I'll give one to each of you," the genie announces.
The first dinosaur thinks hard about what he wants.
"Alright," he says. "I want a thick, juicy, piece of meat."
Instantly, the most succulent, juiciest piece of meat he's ever laid eyes on appears in front of him.
Not to be outdone, the second dinosaur thinks even harder.
"I know! I want a shower of meat!"
Immediately, huge pieces of meat rain down around him.
The third dinosaur, determined he wouldn't be outdone by his friends, thinks even harder than the previous dinosaurs.
"I've got it!" he shouts, puffing out his chest in pride.
"I want a MEATIER shower!"

CHAPTER ONE
-ARIZONA-

What do you call an anxious dino?
A NERVOUS REX.

"Five minutes until your presentation, Arizona. Are you ready?"

Lost in my thoughts, I jumped and barely held back a scream. Spinning around, I came face-to-face with Teresa, the museum curator. She gave me a reassuring smile that did little to calm my frayed nerves.

"Uh, yeah. I'm ready." I was lying, and Teresa likely knew it.

I was as ready to go out in front of the museum's dinner guests as I was to chug a gallon of laxatives. Frankly, there were quite a few things I'd rather do than give tonight's presentation. I'd rather get a paper cut on my cornea and rub salt in it while taking a bath in jalapeño juice, walk barefoot through Legoland after a tornado has scattered sharp Legos over every square inch of property, shave my legs with a chainsaw, fold a fitted sheet, eat a leftover salad, show my mates my middle school yearbook, tap dance in a minefield wearing clown shoes, or use a leaf blower to scatter glitter around my apartment. Heck, I'd even tickle an angry lion's balls with a short stick if it would get me out of tonight's lecture.

Taking a deep, calming breath, I watched Teresa's long, blood-red fingernail tap against the side of her clipboard. The crimson hue of her manicured nails matched the shade of her lipstick with impossible perfection. How did anyone manage to match the two when there were about a zillion shades of both?

I narrowed my eyes in suspicion. Maybe it was Maybelline, or maybe it was magic…

She's human, Ari. There's no magic in this woman, Rez said into the mental bond, not bothering to hide his amusement.

I ignored Rez, which was impressive since his fully shifted T-Rex body currently towered over me. He sounded confident, but he was a man. This might be a type of magic he didn't understand. Like how my ex-boyfriend was confident he had magic fingers that could find the sweet spot in my cave of wonders, but it was a magic he definitely hadn't possessed.

The raptor to my left wheezed out a strangled breath.

Zon, you are supposed to be still and quiet! You two are supposed to be animatronics, not living, breathing dinosaurs. We can't afford for anyone to get suspicious, I hissed through the bond, shooting a warning look at my raptor mate.

Then you should stop entertaining me, Zon retorted. *Your mind is chaotic, but I like it. It's far more amusing than watching TV.*

I rolled my eyes, then turned away from him. The whole 'fated mates' thing was growing on me more with each passing day, but I still wasn't sure I liked having the men in my mind. A girl needed her privacy.

Rez broke into my thoughts. *Why would you need privacy? The link allows us to know your needs instantly.*

And of your desires… You haven't complained about us using the link to please you better during mating. Zon's purr stroked my mind, and my cheeks burned.

"Arizona? Did you hear me?" The curator tilted her head, regarding me worriedly.

"Um, yes. Sorry." I shook my head to clear it of the NSFW images Zon's words had caused to flash through my mind. "Just pre-show nerves."

Teresa laughed and patted my shoulder gently. "It will be fine. Besides, everyone will be in awe of how realistic these dinosaurs appear. I doubt they'll pay much attention to you, anyway." She stared in wide-eyed wonder up at the massive Tyrannosaurus Rex. "It is incredible how far technology has come in the past decade."

"True," I agreed, giving a weak laugh. In my mind, I thought that was exactly what I didn't want. I was trying to pass my very alive shifter mates off as cutting edge, but very much not alive, animatronic dinosaurs. The last thing we needed was for them to be scrutinized.

This was such a bad idea, I groaned into the mental bond. *But you guys just had to get your way.*

You intended to decline the invitation, and we couldn't let that happen. Fate wanted you here, and this was a great first step toward finding what else your grandmother has left for you. Rez sounded so relaxed and confident I almost forgave the guys for pushing me to accept the invite.

Thankfully, Teresa had been more than accommodating of my weird list of requests. Things like covering the costs for my 'team,' a.k.a. mates, to travel with me, booking reservations in a pig-friendly hotel, and most importantly, absolutely no touching the dinosaurs. After explaining this rule was to prevent oils from human skin causing accidental damage to the materials used to create our dinosaur skin, Teresa had accepted the condition without a fuss. I was also being reimbursed for the cost of a large storage warehouse I'd needed to rent in order to store my 'robotic' dinosaurs away from prying eyes.

Even with all the precautions, my body was pretty much vibrating with anxiety and worry. It's good that overthinking things doesn't burn calories. Otherwise, I'd be dead.

Rez snorted, the gust of wind blowing my hair wildly around my face until I looked like I'd just crawled out of a well. Teresa's hair, on the other hand, remained perfect. Not a single strand of her dark hair was out of place. It had been swept up in an effortless chignon that gave off a vibe of graceful elegance. If I tried that hairstyle, I'd be giving off the vibes of a lady living in a shoe with too many kids who survived on black coffee and insanity.

Teresa exuded confidence with her perfect hair, skillfully tailored emerald green pantsuit, and death-defying stiletto heels. She was everything I needed to embody if I hoped to get through this evening without blowing my cover.

Summoning my courage, I peeked out the doorway that led from the staff area out to the museum's well-manicured garden. Air hissed out of my lungs.

"This is a private dinner party? There have to be almost a hundred tables out there!" My hands began to shake. Tiki torches lit up the garden, with staff bustling around in white tuxedos with a pink plumeria boutonniere attached to each of the lapels. Guests mingled around circle tables wearing leis and snagging champagne glasses or pina coladas served in coconuts.

Teresa checked her watch. "Yes. Sadly, several of the guests canceled, so it is a bit smaller than usual." Taking a step toward me, she squeezed my shoulder and gave me a warm, if a little distracted, smile. "You'll do fine, Arizona. Just treat it like you're giving a tour to a group of school kids."

Was that supposed to be helpful? Talking to forty kids was a lot different from talking to over two hundred adults. Kids were easily distracted when you didn't want to answer their questions. Adults were a lot harder to distract.

Warm arms wrapped around my waist, pulling me against a warm chest.

I didn't need to look to know who was hugging me. The

moment he touched me, my anxiety eased, making it a little easier to take a deep breath. "Jack! You made it back in time!"

"Stop worrying, Arizona. You've rehearsed this a thousand times." Jack leaned down and kissed my cheek.

Knowing I had backup in the form of a human if things took a bad turn was exactly the reassurance I needed.

"Not a chance I would miss this." Jack chuckled.

A happy oink had my eyes darting to the ground. There, at Jack's feet, was Albert's familiar light blue crate.

"Why is he here?" I yelped. Adorable as the little pig was, this was the last place he needed to be right now.

"The hotel had to move our room due to an electrical issue on our floor. But they hadn't finished cleaning the new room from the last guest. The staff stored our luggage, but I didn't think Albert would appreciate being crammed into the stuffy storeroom." Jack shrugged. "So I brought him with me."

Albert gave an adorable oink and bobbed his head.

Rez snorted and took a cautious step away. Zon's long tail whacked the wall, sending a rain of plaster showering onto the ground as he stomped his clawed feet in agitation. Both dinos eyed the tiny crate with unease as though it held the world's most dangerous animal.

It does. One day you will discover the truth about your Albert. Zon's words were a whisper in my mind.

I rolled my eyes, but didn't have time to form a response. It was show time.

"Let's go, Arizona!" Teresa called over her shoulder as she headed out into the party.

Reluctantly wiggling out of Jack's embrace, I moved to follow her. Rez and Zon lumbered quickly behind me, preferring the crowd overstaying near Albert Einswine.

Turning, I blew a kiss toward Jack. "Make sure he doesn't get out of that crate. The last thing we need tonight is a surprise appearance from the little ham."

Jack laughed.

CHAPTER TWO
-ARIZONA-

What's a dinosaur's favorite drink?
REX ON THE BEACH!

After being introduced to the museum's dinner guests, I plunged straight into my presentation on the importance of preserving the past to teach future generations. The sooner I got this over with, the sooner I could head back to my hotel room.

Walking around Zon's raptor form, I spoke about exciting new discoveries being made by paleontologists every year. Teresa gave me a thumbs up when I emphasized that with every bit of new information, the entire world would learn more about the magnificent beasts who walked the earth so long ago. She probably planned to use that point to convince the guests to reach deeper into their pockets to support the museum.

I pulled a tiny remote from my pocket and aimed it in

Rez's direction while pressing some buttons. Rez responded with a flick of his tail. The crowd clapped in delight, falling for the deception that this huge T-Rex was controlled by a tiny remote. A remote that didn't even have a working battery in it. If only they knew the truth about the dinos or the fact that the remote had been dug out of Jack's kitchen junk drawer. Jack thought it belonged to a remote-control car he'd owned a dozen or so years ago, but he couldn't remember for sure.

Turning to the DJ, I nodded. A second later, the beginning of *Dinosaur* by Kesha blared through the speakers. The tyrannosaurus bobbed his head in time to the music. Laughter rippled through the audience. Not wanting to be outdone, the raptor turned his back to me and shifted his butt from side to side. Cheers and whistles rang out from the guests.

I looked out over the semi-circle of tables around me. Every single person was watching the dinos, their eyes sparkling with excitement. No one clicked away on cell phones, and the plates of food in front of each person had barely been touched. These adults held an almost childlike wonder on their faces as they watched the dinosaurs dance —if you could call it that.

To my relief, both dinos kept their movements stiff and slightly jerky, helping to sell the idea of them being robotic. When the DJ cut off the music, I clicked the remote, and just like we'd practiced, Rez's massive head lowered to mine. The tyrannosaurus gave a harsh snort that sent a gust of wind through my hair, causing it to fly wildly around my face. This sent the crowd into a fresh burst of laughter.

That wasn't part of our routine, I grumbled through the link, desperately running my fingers through my out-of-control hair.

That is true. Rez's chest rumbled with laughter. *But it was funny.*

Mistaking the T-Rex's sound of amusement as a threatening growl, the crowd gasped, leaning back in their chairs as their primal survival instincts belatedly showed up at the party.

"How cool is that?" I smiled, trying to calm the anxiety I saw flashing through several faces. "Thanks to scientific advancements in technology, we've been able to replicate the sounds it is believed dinosaurs would have made when they walked the earth. Pretty impressive, huh?"

The crowd murmured their agreement, and I decided to jump straight into discussing the Tyrannosaurus Rex and various raptor species. I walked around my dinosaurs throughout my talk, occasionally clicking a button on my remote to keep up the illusion I was the one controlling the all-too-real dinos.

My presentation lasted an hour, and despite my misgivings, much to my surprise, it went off without a hitch. Giving the guests an awkward curtsy that I would definitely be overthinking at 3 a.m., I handed my mic to Teresa and made my escape.

Almost.

Teresa caught my arm, pulling me to an abrupt halt.

"Thank you, Arizona! Before we let you escape, does anyone in the audience have a question for our special guest?"

I stiffened, and my blood turned to ice. This hadn't been part of the plan. In fact, I specifically told Teresa I wasn't open to questions due to company policy. And by company, I had, of course, meant the shell design company Jack had created for us to use as a cover. Dinovation. Jack had used one of his shady contacts to ensure the company was set up properly and that it would hold up under scrutiny. I guess it paid off to have an ex-detective as a mate.

To my horror, at least two dozen hands shot into the air. Teresa turned to me with a beaming smile and handed me the mic. She quickly disappeared into the crowd before I could protest.

"Pluck my sucking luck," I mumbled under my breath.

Hard as I tried, I couldn't figure a way out of my predicament without coming across as a complete Snatch-squash. Grinding my teeth together in annoyance, I pointed at a woman in the crowd and, one by one, began answering questions.

Thankfully, most of the guests enjoyed the continuous flow of red wine, and most of their questions were easier to answer than the questions asked by third-grade students during school tours. I breezed through nearly every question in under fifteen minutes, and my confidence grew with each one.

It all came to a screeching halt when a gentleman in a dark suit stood. Without bothering to raise his hand, he asked, "Can you explain how Dinovation has been able to find funding for a multimillion-dollar project in only a few weeks since its formation? And for that matter, how was Dinovation able to create these dinosaur prototypes on such short notice?"

There was no way I could answer his question with the truth, so I tried to make a joke. "I believe I'd find myself fired before midnight if I shared our secret to success."

The audience chuckled, but the man was undeterred. "I highly doubt that, Ms. Charcoal." He took a step forward, and my stomach knotted at the smirk on his sharp-featured face.

"Dinovation wouldn't allow just anyone to run around playing with such valuable company assets. I've done my research, and I suspect you're fairly high up in the company. Which means your job is quite secure, regardless of what you say."

Trying to appear calmer than I felt, I wheezed out a breathless laugh. "What can I say? I'm good at my job."

Mister Rudey-McRude-Face snorted. "Oh, yes. I assume you have to be good at something since your resume isn't exactly befitting your sudden climb from janitor to your current position." He strode to stand directly in front of me, stopping when his chest was mere inches from my face.

It was a display of dominance meant to put me in my place, and Zon wasn't having it. The raptor's pupils narrowed to menacing slits, and his jaws snapped as he circled the arrogant man.

"Cute." The man seemed unconcerned by Zon and

turned his cold blue eyes back on me. "I'd like to make you —I mean, your bosses"—he raised a brow, making it clear he didn't believe I had a boss—"an offer. With more funding and a bit of polish, I believe these dinosaurs could appear far more realistic."

Forgetting all about being irritated, he was doing this in front of an entire audience. My mouth fell open in pure disbelief. Was he serious? How much more lifelike did he want my living, breathing dinosaurs to be? If it hadn't been for the whole 'magic isn't real and dinosaurs are extinct' belief, the whole world would have been pretty adamant about it. I'd have thought I was on an episode of *Candid Camera*.

The man held out his business card. I was still trying to process his impressively high levels of both arrogance and ignorance, and my fingers took the card before my brain could tell them not to. Glancing down at the card, I saw there was only a phone number and a name—Bartholomew Burkhardt.

Taking advantage of my distraction, Bartholomew stepped around me and reached out a hand to touch Zon's shoulder. The raptor spun out of the man's reach with an angry hiss.

The man laughed along with the audience, but I didn't miss the annoyance as it flashed across his face. "It's impressive how well you're able to control their move-ments. I'd love to let my tech guys spend some time with these two. With their experience, I'm sure they could have both dinosaurs performing far more complex actions."

Zon's hiss hadn't deterred Bartholomew from reaching out to touch the dinosaurs yet again.

This time, I was faster and stepped between him and Rez's scale-covered flank. "Sir, Teresa made it clear at the beginning of the presentation that the dinosaurs were not to be handled in order to prevent damage. I need you to step back. Please." I ground out the last word, trying to hang onto my quickly crumbling professional facade.

Let me eat him, Zon snarled in the link.

Not worth it. This human is all calories and no substance. Rez blew out an angry breath.

Bartholomew's eyes flashed with something dark, sending an icy shiver racing down my spine. This man was trying to appear easy-going and affable, but there was a coldness lurking beneath his friendly exterior.

He wasn't a man who was used to being told no. Well, that was too freaking bad.

Let's be real. I wasn't used to saying no. But with the two predators pressing close to my back, that one-syllable word rolled easily off my tongue. "I'm happy to discuss things further at a later date, but I cannot allow you to touch the dinosaurs. If I did, everyone would want to touch them, and my bosses wouldn't be pleased."

"Get this through your head. I don't take no for an answer when I want something." Dingle-Douche had given up pretending to be civil and stuck his pointed finger in my face to emphasize his words.

Worst. Mistake. Ever.

Rez lowered his massive head until the cool scales of his

nose pressed against my back, and his hot breath blew against my sweat-soaked skin. Zon's muscles tensed as he prepared to launch himself if Bartholomew touched me. The crowd's laughter died away, and the entire waitstaff stood frozen as they watched the little showdown.

Out of the corner of my eye, I spotted Jack heading toward me with murder on his face. It wasn't just the dinosaurs who were protective of me. Jack's hands were clenched, and as he grew closer, I could see his jaw muscle tick. Teresa hurried behind Jack, trying and failing to keep up with his long strides.

It was about rubber-ducking time! Jack was exactly the type of backup I needed to tidy up this situation. Both dinos were showing incredible control over their beasts, but I knew it wouldn't last long.

Rez can eat him in one bite. No mess. I've seen him do it, Zon supplied unhelpfully. His tail twitched, and the long, sharp nail of his right foot tapped the ground. It was a warning that Zon was losing control.

I wanted to reassure my mates and help them calm their beasts, but the world around me seemed to slow when I caught sight of something that struck fear into the deepest part of my soul.

Like a scene straight out of my worst nightmare, Albert came racing around the corner of the brick building. His little hooves slid out from under him as he took the turn too fast and rolled across the grass. He didn't let the tumble slow him down, though, as he rolled back to his feet and kept running.

This was exactly the type of backup I didn't need.

As the pink pork of perdition charged toward us, he released an adorable squeal that struck fear in the hearts of all who heard it.

Fine. It struck fear in only three hearts—two shifters and myself.

Seeing the terror on my face, Jack spun and dove toward Albert. Without missing a beat, the pudgy pigskin dodged Jack's hands and, digging his tiny hooves into the soft museum lawn, Albert Einswine barreled straight toward me... and my dinos.

CHAPTER THREE
-ARIZONA-

What do you call a dinosaur fart?
A BLAST FROM THE PAST!

"M ove!" I screamed at the butthole who'd caused this mess. Bartholomew might be a pile of crap, but I didn't want him to die.

"Who do you think you are, talking to me like that?" Bartholomew bellowed, reaching out to grab my arm.

Not having time to explain the danger he was in, I threw my body against his, knocking us both to the ground. Air whistled past us as Zon's raptor launched toward the spot Bartholomew had been standing. The moment Albert squealed, Zon's control snapped like a rubber band. As though a switch had been flipped, the dinos were now running on instinct, and that wasn't a good thing for the man who dared to harass their mate.

I'm barely holding back my beast. I'll turn this arrogant fool

19

inside out for daring to touch you. Rez's roar of displeasure caused dishes to rattle and the ground to vibrate beneath our feet. It was a terrifying sound that would echo in my ears for hours. The T-Rex swung around to where Bartholomew was staggering to his feet, confusion and anger twisting his features into an ugly mask.

I truly believe my generally gentle tyrannosaurus mate would have turned the jerkwad into a chew toy if not for Albert picking that precise moment to dash in front of Rez. Spooked, the T-Rex stumbled backward, barely managing to catch his balance, and not before taking out one of the elegant white canopies draped above the guests' tables.

People screamed, scrambling to get away. Women cried out as their spiked heels caught in long silk-skirted gowns, sending them tumbling to the ground. The beautifully prepared dinner was forgotten as tables toppled, and filet mignon, roast pork, and roasted vegetables were tossed across the lawn. The metal awnings holding up the white canopies screeched as the steel bent each time Rez's tail slammed into them.

Through the chaos, I spotted Teresa. Her hair had escaped from its elegant bun, leaving her hair to fall free around her face, and the knees of her suit were dirty; she must have fallen to the ground at some point. Even so, she stood calm, her back straight as she directed the pale, trembling guests inside the museum. As long as we could keep the dinosaurs from rampaging through the building, the guests should be safe.

With Teresa handling the people, I turned my attention

to finding my pig, knowing the dino shifters would never calm down with him running free. Dodging overturned tables and Rez's swinging tail, I searched frantically for the tiny terror. I didn't have to hunt for him long. Albert ran by me, giving a joyful donkey kick with his back legs as he streaked between the last few guests, still making their way to safety.

Using the table skirt as cover, Jack and I squatted and rushed after Albert, hoping to catch him before one of the dinos stepped on him or he pushed them to their breaking point, and they decided to start attacking everything in sight.

Careful to keep one eye on the dino shifters, I anxiously watched as they alternated between hunting down Bartholomew and then escaping from the terrifying game of peek-a-boo warfare Albert had decided to launch against them.

I had to admit, Albert was doing an incredible job of keeping the dinosaurs from rampaging through the guests, and he was deterring them from crashing straight through the side of the museum. But there was no doubt that his presence was fraying the shifters' nerves and causing them to be more on edge with each second that ticked by.

If we could just catch Albert, and Teresa got Bartholomew out of the dinos' line of sight, I might have a chance of calming my shifter mates. Possibly.

Catching Albert proved far more challenging than I'd thought. He preferred being a pig-in-a-blanket on the couch watching cartoons, so when had he found the time to hone his track skills? No matter how hard Jack and I tried, we failed to catch Albert.

Every time we thought we had him, he'd dodge our hands and disappear under a nearby table. Stranger still, a heartbeat later, he'd pop out from beneath a different table across the room… and he had the uncanny ability to pick the table that just happened to be closest to one of the dino shifters.

Trying to escape Albert darting across the grass, Zon leaped on top of the single long serving table that had been stacked until it overflowed with various culinary delights. Unable to hold the weight of a full-grown male raptor, the table collapsed, sending Zon and the various dishes crashing to the ground.

Albert, predictably, picked that moment to make another appearance. Dashing through the scattered remains of dinner covering the lawn, he happily snatched up his favorite treat as he rushed past the stunned raptor lying on the ground amid the museum's ruined feast. Without slowing, and with the shiny apple clamped firmly in his mouth, Albert raced toward Rez, who'd headed toward the museum door Bartholomew had disappeared through.

Just as Albert sprung into the air at Rez, I snatched him midair, barely preventing him from becoming a groundhog beneath the T-Rex's foot. Clutching Albert against me, and with my trembling legs unable to hold me up, I sank into a chair that had miraculously escaped destruction.

My chest ached, and blood pounded in my ears. Gasping in deep lungfuls of humid night air, and heart filled with trepidation, I slowly took in the scene around me. Three of the four canopies that circled the presentation area had been flipped over or collapsed. The fourth was still standing, but the white fabric top had been slashed through by sharp T-Rex claws. The pale fabric billowed in the warm breeze, reminding me of a white flag waving in sad surrender.

To my immense relief, there were no injured guests or dead bodies strewn about the grassy lawn. My gaze shot to the museum. Through the glass windows, I could make out a few guests holding cell phones in the direction of the dinosaurs and destruction in the courtyard. Several other guests were talking to Teresa, their hands waving wildly while she nodded calmly in response. Were they demanding my arrest for endangering their lives? Were they calling in the military to euthanize my shifter mates? There was no way I'd be able to reimburse the museum for the damage to the party, let alone the emotional distress to the guests.

The world tilted and swirled as thoughts of being on the run for the rest of my life threatened to overwhelm me. How could I keep Jack, Albert Einswine, and two probably unstable dinosaurs safe? How was I supposed to hide a freaking Tyrannosaurus Rex? The only thing I'd ever successfully hidden was important documents, and that was by accident! I'd put them in a safe place so they wouldn't get lost, and they'd been so safe I hadn't been able to find them again.

Looking toward the dinosaurs, I snorted. There wasn't a

chance I'd accidentally lose them. Both dinos were still inside the circle of grass dedicated to my presentation. I'd half expected the shifters to be crushing Porsches and Mercedes in the parking lot on their way to destroy half of downtown Dallas, or have destroyed half the museum in their anger while trying to find Bartholomew.

The dinosaurs' flanks heaved, and they drew in one harsh breath after another. I knew why they'd stayed. Because Albert had kept them there, guiding them away from fleeing guests and buildings. Sure, he'd caused part of the chaos, but he'd also herded them like a pro and kept them in an area where the damage they caused was minimal compared to how things could have ended. And he'd distracted them from going after Bartholomew, which was no small feat, considering how badly they had tried to get to him.

Albert's tiny body quivered against mine, and glancing down, I caught the shine in his eyes. He wasn't afraid. No, I suspected the troublemaker was shaking from exertion and excitement. The crisp red apple was still firmly clutched in his jaws, and adding to the absurdity of the evening, a brightly colored flower lei, probably from the scattered remains of the table decor, was wrapped around his neck.

Sinking to the ground, I began to laugh. It didn't take long for my giggles to turn into sobs, though, as the stress and panic of the evening overwhelmed me. My brain was struggling to cope with the deluge of emotions I'd felt in the span of an hour, and the terror of my unknown future.

"Hey. Shh…" Jack lifted me into his arms. "Let's get out of here."

"What about Rez and Zon?" I hiccuped.

Without breaking stride or setting me down, Jack reached out with one hand and yanked a tablecloth from a table that had managed to escape the devastation. The fabric slid free without rattling a single plate or tipping over any of the wineglasses.

"Please tell me you aren't freaking magical, too?" My grandmother had done a number on my life, and I needed Jack to be my 'normal' anchor amidst the paranormal world I'd recently been sucked into.

"I'm beginning to think I'm the only ordinary thing in your life." Jack chuckled and tossed the white cloth over my chest. "Keep Albert out of sight. Rez and Zon are on overload right now, and if we want to get any sleep tonight, they need a chance to calm down."

Nodding, I tucked the fabric around my upper body, hiding my pet potbelly from view. Albert didn't seem to care and happily munched on his prize. One problem taken care of, I focused my attention on my two shifter mates.

Rez? Zon? Are you two okay? I tried to make my voice as soothing as possible in the link, unsure if the men or the beast inside them held more control of their minds at that moment. What I really wanted to ask was if they were calm enough not to attack someone, but I also didn't think reminding them about Bartholomew was wise.

Fine, Rez responded, his voice tight. His labored

breathing slowed, and he locked his gaze on me. *Need time to gain control.*

I looked toward the raptor, and my heart tripped as fear caused it to forget its rhythm. The raptor's wild, glowing eyes locked onto me. I wasn't an expert on dinosaurs, but this didn't really seem like the sort of look a loving mate might give. Nope, this was the look of a predator with ravenous hunger. Surely, he wasn't going to—

The raptor lowered his head and, like a lion stalking a gazelle, stepped silently across the ground toward me. The calculated, slow movements were somehow a hundred times more terrifying than if he'd chosen to run toward me at full speed.

Reflexively, I squeezed Albert tighter against my chest, never taking my eyes off the raptor who seemed to be hunting me. Shifters didn't hurt their mates. What could have gone so wrong that now he wanted to attack me?

And Zon? Is he still, um... in control? I couldn't stop myself from asking Rez the question, even though I already knew the answer, as Zon continued to stalk slowly toward me. If he didn't hurry up, my life wasn't going to flash before my eyes. It was going to have time to play like an entire feature film.

No. He's not. Rez didn't elaborate. Instead, he released a deafening roar and stepped between us, using his body to block the raptor's view of where Jack stood with me in his arms.

Since I'd met the guys, I'd believed Zon would back down if given an order by Rez, so when the raptor responded with a vicious roar of his own, I knew we were in serious trouble. Zon lunged for Rez, his jaws snapping with a forceful crack that echoed against the brick of the nearby buildings.

"We need to do something," Jack whispered.

Twisting around in his arms to stare up at him, I gave him an are-you-serious look. "You do remember they are very real dinosaurs who have humans on their food chain, right?"

"But we can't stand here and do nothing!" Jack protested, raising his voice to be heard over the dinos' increasingly loud roars.

"Agreed. Now run!" I screamed, clinging to Jack as he lurched to the side to avoid Rez's tail.

None of this made sense, but in the confusion of the moment, my exhausted brain couldn't seem to come up with any other reason for Zon's feral behavior. I was new to being mated to shifters, and I didn't understand enough about how a shifter's beast brain worked once it took full control. All I knew was my survival instincts told me I was being chased by a predator, and I needed to escape.

Catching his balance, Jack raced to the parking lot and away from the battling pair. My relief was short-lived. Peeking over Jack's shoulder, I witnessed the precise moment both dinos spotted us making a hasty retreat.

The raptor yanked his teeth free from the T-Rex's thigh and leaped toward us. Rez snarled and spun to follow, all the while snapping at the smaller dinosaur, who was quickly closing the gap between us.

"Are they coming after us?" Jack shouted, not bothering to slow down and check for himself.

"Yep." I chewed my lip.

"They won't hurt you, though. You're their mate!" Jack breathed, sprinting faster across the lawn.

"Of course not," I lied, not seeing any reason to worry him more. Our deaths would be instantaneous and mostly painless. Probably. Maybe?

Zon was faster than Rez, but Rez was bigger. Taking several earthquake-inducing steps, Rez managed to get in front of the raptor. The massive T-Rex lowered his head and opened his mouth.

Yep. I was about to be the proud owner of an eight-foot plot of land… in a cemetery.

Far more delicately than I'd have thought him capable of being, the T-Rex snagged Jack's shirt between his teeth and lifted him, with me cradled tight in his arms, off the ground. Rez stood to his full height, carefully keeping us away from the hissing raptor snapping in rage at his heels. Not ready to give up, Zon continued to circle Rez, alternating between angry-sounding clicks and rumbling snarls.

"Is he going to be okay, Rez?" My voice wobbled, and hot tears burned my eyes. Would I ever be held in Zon's arms again? Would I get to see his cheeky smile when he teased me or the heat in his eyes when we made love? Or was he going to be stuck like this forever? "Zon looks like he wants to eat me."

He wants to eat you, but not in the way you are thinking, Rez's deep voice answered in my mind.

The giant shifter's chest rumbled and mistaking it as a threat, Jack's arms tightened around me, eliciting an irritated grunt from Albert.

A strange male threatened you, Ari. That calls out to the most primal part of our beasts and demands we prove ourselves as worthy mates. We are driven to eliminate all threats, make sure you're protected, and then reinforce our bond by mating until you are satisfied and can no longer walk straight. Rez's voice in the link was stilted, still not entirely his own.

Will you two be able to regain control? I glanced down at Zon but quickly looked away when the height made me dizzy.

Rez moved through the parking lot and toward the warehouse storage building. *Yes. Eventually. The pig's unexpected attack added to our beast's frenzy. I was able to maintain control. Zon could not. He will calm down when we are away from this place. But when he does shift to his human form, the beast will likely still control much of his mind. We need to keep him away from you. Otherwise, you will be in for a rough experience.*

The guys were incredible lovers, and the very idea of Zon not holding back had my temperature rising and a wave of need washing through me.

I didn't mind a rough ride. Besides, I'd always thought it would be fun to be a cowgirl.

CHAPTER FOUR
-ARIZONA-

What do you get if you cross a T-Rex with explosives?
DINO-MITE.

T hankfully, the warehouse was less than two blocks from the museum. We were able to take a nearly vacant backstreet rather than taking the busy main road. The quiet road, combined with the late hour, meant we were able to avoid gawking drivers, flashing cell phone cameras, and angry car horns.

It was a relief, since I wasn't sure how much more stimulation my dino mates could take without rampaging—again. Unshed tears stung my eyes. I wasn't sure how much more of tonight I could take.

It was taking every bit of energy I had to keep my magic under control. That was the last thing we needed. At best, the flare of energy would rile my dino mates more, and half the city might end up destroyed. At worst, I'd detonate and destroy half the city by myself.

Rez must have sensed my distress because he sighed, blowing a harsh puff of air through his nose.

Jack jerked, his arms tightening around me. "Is he angry?"

Rez hadn't said anything through our bond since he'd warned me about Zon, but our minds were still connected. I wasn't very skilled with exactly how the mind link voodoo worked, but with each passing day, I was getting a tiny bit better at it. Closing my eyes, I imagined the delicate threads connecting us and felt for Rez's emotions.

"No. He's—" I hesitated, squeezing my eyes closed tighter as I tried to focus. "I think Rez is frustrated? Or maybe he's worried?"

"Great. That makes two of us," Jack mumbled, so low he probably didn't think I'd heard him.

The human doesn't trust us when we are shifted into our beasts, Rez finally said through the link, his voice flat but holding no judgment.

Slowly opening my eyelids, I tilted my head to peek down at the ground. Zon's glowing eyes were locked on me, his long tongue flicking across the dagger-sharp teeth lining his reptilian mouth.

Rez, can you blame Jack? Zon is still circling us like a hungry shark who smells blood in the water. I think he's even salivating a bit. I tried to stifle my worry, but it was futile.

My magic began to vibrate through me as a tiny crack formed in the inner wall I was using to keep it contained.

What if Rez was wrong? What if Zon was too far gone to come back to me?

Still. Here. Baby.

The words brushed against my mind like the soft beat of butterfly wings. Each syllable was clipped, as though spoken by a parrot who was still learning to mimic human speech. But it didn't matter, because I recognized the voice. *Zonkut.*

I stole another glance down to find the raptor watching me as he wove his way between Rez's massive, clawed feet. Catching my searching gaze, Zon released a rapid-fire string of clicks and chirps. Sadly, I couldn't discern if he was excited or agitated.

Both. Rez snorted out another gust of air. *Zonkut wishes for me to walk faster. He knows I am purposely moving slowly. I am giving him time to calm his beast, but the delay is greatly irritating him.*

To my surprise, my usually serious mate slowed his steps even more until he was moving in theatrically slow motion.

Are you trying to make him angrier? I gasped into the link.

Zon is anxious to mate with you. I'm unwilling to fight him and risk accidentally killing him, or you. That means Zon will get to have you first tonight. But he is not the only one struggling to control his beast, and I'm not eager to watch him breed you when I want the same thing. Rez followed that revelation up by snarling at Zon.

"What is Rez doing? Don't tell me they are both losing

it. He better not drop us!" Jack's deep baritone voice rose as the dinos' hisses grew louder.

"Rez is antagonizing Zon because he's jealous. Logically, he knows Zon is less stable, but his dino doesn't exactly want to share right now." I breathed out a sigh of relief when the warehouse came into view. *Almost there.*

There was a long pause before Jack's lips brushed my ear. "Do you think this will work long-term?"

"Will what work?" I asked, with a sinking stomach. But I knew what he meant.

"Firefly, having one dinosaur shifter as a mate is a prehistoric feat." Jack's voice was gentle.

I ignored the stupid pun, knowing Jack was trying to soften the blow of what he was about to say.

He continued. "But having two shifters as mates and trying to juggle their needs as men- and shifters—it's a lot to ask of you."

Anger crackled inside me, and my magic bubbled up. The telltale scent of ozone wafted into the air. Every time I'd smelled it before, it had spelled trouble. I needed to calm down.

Taking a steadying breath, I leaned away from Jack so I could look him in the eye. When I spoke, my voice was soft. "Are you unhappy? You don't have to stay, Jack. I told you from the start that sharing wasn't going to be easy for any of us. It is going to take some getting used to."

"Ari, I'm not feeling jealous or neglected. I'm worried. These two men could rip you to shreds, and there isn't anything I could do to stop them. I don't want to watch you get hurt, or worse, watch you die." Jack didn't bother to hide the raw emotion in his voice.

"I'll be fine. Probably sore, but fine." I tried to sound confident and reassuring, but the truth was, I had no idea what was in store for me.

Jack's reply was cut off by Rez's loud snort. The T-Rex had paused in front of the large cargo bay door and was impatiently waiting for us to open it.

The dark alley made it a challenge, but after fumbling through all of Jack's pockets, I found the electronic key fob. My fingers trembled, nearly causing me to drop it. Finally managing to hit the correct button, we waited while the two-story tall metal garage door slid upward with a series of angry creaks and shudders.

Once the door was out of the way, Rez lowered his massive head and carried us, still dangling from his mouth, into the warehouse. I quickly pressed another button, and the metal door began to drop, protesting with a set of bellowing groans and metal-against-metal shrieks.

When the racket quieted, we were left standing in pitch-black darkness. There were very few windows in the building, and they'd all been covered in dark paint to keep any curious teenagers from peeking inside.

I wasn't sure what had been stored in the museum previously, but based on the reinforced steel doors and covered windows, they hadn't wanted anyone to know what was going on in here, which suited us just fine.

Zon's excited clicks and rumbles echoed through the

empty warehouse, causing blood to roar in my ears and my magic to flare.

We both knew what was coming.

A clever girl would run for her life right about now, but I knew I wasn't going anywhere. For better or for worse, these were my mates.

CLICKING at the buttons on the remote, I switched on the overhead lights and fans.

Tell Jack to set you on the ground. The moment your feet touch the ground, I will lift him out of the way again, Rez rumbled into the link.

I relayed the message to Jack, who paled. "Maybe we should just keep you out of Zon's reach until he has calmed down?"

Watching my raptor mate, I shook my head. "Zon is only going to get more worked up until he burns himself out or is lost to his beast. I can't risk Zon hurting himself."

I kissed Jack's cheek, hoping to reassure him that everything would work itself out.

Dropping his head, Rez lowered us so that Jack was able to set me on my feet. The instant my shoes touched the ground, Rez yanked his head back, hauling Jack away from any accidental raptor-induced injuries.

With my magic vibrating through me like I was a

battery-operated back massager, I turned on my heel to face Zon... and choked on my scream.

The raptor rushed at me with his claws extended, ready to slice me in two. I watched in horror as his powerful muscles bunched, and he sprung into the air toward me. His eyes glowed, and I braced for the impact of his sharp talons on my skin.

Boy oh boy, was the medical examiner who did my autopsy going to have a hard time explaining how someone in the twenty-first century had died by a dinosaur attack!

Bracing for impact, I was stunned when Zon stopped midair. Hitting the ground hard, he twisted around. We both stared at Rez's massive foot... which was pressed down on the raptor's tail.

SHIFT, Rez ordered through the mind link, his T-Rex rumbling a warning that shook the walls.

Zon jerked forward, trying to free his pinned tail. When that failed, the raptor released a vicious hiss.

SHIFT!

I winced as Rez's harsh command roared into the link.

The stubborn raptor ignored the order, still desperately trying to get to me. A feral hunger glowed in his eyes.

You will kill her. Shift now, or I will remove our mate from the warehouse. Rez delivered the threat with a calmness that sent goosebumps trailing across my skin.

Zonkut released a furious barrage of clicks and growls.

"Did he just cuss you out?" Jack asked the T-Rex, who still held him by the shirt like a mother cat holding a kitten.

Rez snorted, clearly unimpressed by Zon's tantrum.

Coming to the conclusion that the T-Rex wasn't going to change his mind, Zon's beast gave a last snarl and caved to Rez's demand. The air shimmered and rippled with magic as the raptor shifted back into his gorgeous blonde-haired human form. My ovaries swooned, just like they always did when I looked at my sinfully sexy mates.

With his tail gone, Zon was freed from Rez's foot. Wasting no time, he moved to close the distance between us. As he neared me, I could see the thin slits of Zon's pupils. His body might be human, but it was 100 percent beast that watched me from Zon's glowing eyes.

The single brain cell that oversaw my survival instincts suddenly remembered its sole purpose—keeping me alive —and burst into action. I stumbled away from the powerful man stalking toward me, only to trip over a stray soda can.

My arms pinwheeled, and I stumbled into the jungle of thick chains that hung from the ceiling and coiled on the floor. I was caught in their snare as they wrapped around me like serpents.

When I finally stopped falling, the tangle of chains held me suspended above the floor, like a fly in a spiderweb.

I wiggled, trying to free myself as Zon stalked toward me. It was futile. The steel chains were impossibly heavy. Back when the warehouse had been in use, the chains and pulleys were used to lift engines and heavy machinery, so my struggle did little to move them.

Knowing I couldn't unwrap or wiggle out of the chains before Zonkut reached me, I curled my fingers around the links and braced myself. If I'd expected him to free me from the tangle, I would have been disappointed.

My shifter mate had something else in mind. Zon's hands gripped my thighs, pulling me forward. Held up by the chains, my body swung toward him.

He didn't stop until I was upside down, my long hair almost brushing the concrete floor. If the spider web of steel holding me decided to release me in my current position, I'd hit the ground with skull-rattling force.

My crazy mate gripped my thighs tighter and hooked my legs over his shoulders. Happy for the added security, I tightened my legs, stabilizing myself. With the silver chains wrapped around my limbs as I hung from Zon's neck, I probably looked like a circus performer about to execute a breathtaking stunt.

But it was Zon who did a stunt that stole the air from my lungs. Sliding his left hand between my legs, he ripped away my thong. The sharp snap of fabric elicited a gasp of pain from me, but it quickly turned to a moan of pleasure when Zon's mouth pressed to my soaked slit.

While I dangled like a marionette tangled in her own strings, Zon's tongue plunged deep inside me. The man wasn't playing around; he was devouring me.

His tongue lengthened, stretching me as it sank deeper inside me. It twisted and flicked as he licked up every last drop of my slick he could find. The combination of friction and stroking was too much, and I cried out as my orgasm ripped through my flushed body.

Ignoring my whimpers, Zon continued to lap up the

evidence of my desire.

My overly sensitive body trembled with violent after-shocks as his tongue continued to delve into my silky heat.

"Zon," I half-cried and half-moaned.

He responded with a rumbling growl.

Just when I thought I'd lose my mind if his tongue stroked me one more time, Zon shifted positions. Dropping my wobbly legs from around his shoulders, he released his hold on my thighs, letting me swing away from him.

"AH!" I screamed as my body turned weightless at the sudden drop.

My cry was cut off when the chains stopped my fall with a hard jerk, supporting my weight in a makeshift swing. I clung to thick links, unable to even think of freeing myself while in motion.

Zon had other plans.

Plans that didn't involve me escaping my bonds.

Reaching out, he grabbed the chains above me. Zon's biceps flexed as he swung me forward, impaling me on his engorged erection.

Once again, there was no gentle teasing. My mouth fell open in shock, but no sound came out. Zon pushed the chains back, and my body slid away from his.

Wasting no time, he pulled the chains toward him again. This time, his hard length plunged inside me until I was almost certain it hit the back of my throat.

My dress had slid up over my hips thanks to being held upside down, and the chains dug into my skin. Our makeshift sex swing was far from comfortable, and my skin would definitely show marks from it tomorrow, but I didn't care.

Zon found a rhythm, rocking me back and forth as he roughly buried himself inside me. Our breathing grew more ragged with each stroke. It was rough, erotic, and sexy as a frick.

As my blonde shifter thrust inside me, I found it impossible to look away from his stunning green eyes. Predatory-slitted pupils watched me. Zon's beast was barely contained. Why was that so hot? My stomach clenched, sending a wave of heat between my legs to coat his cock.

My magic sparked, humming around me. Zon's eyes flickered, and his nostrils flared as he took in the combined scent of my arousal and magic. His chest vibrated with something between a purr and a groan.

It was my undoing. Was there anything sexier than seeing the raw lust and desire shimmering in your mate's eyes as he looked at you?

My lust burned hotter, and my need coiled tighter each time his thick erection sank inside me. I was rushing toward my climax and couldn't do anything but try to survive the ride.

One more stroke—

I was yanked from the precipice of pleasure as Zon's arm wrapped around my waist and flipped me over. He was maneuvering me in the chains as though I weighed nothing.

"Zon!" I yelped, dizzy from the quick shift of position.

I blinked furiously, trying to focus my blurred vision.

His only response was to slam himself deep inside me. This time, his length began to grow, shifting into something I'd only felt once before... when Rez claimed me as his mate.

I moaned, the pain from being stretched blending with pleasure. My inner hussy was delighted to once again experience this unique bonus that came with a dino shifter as your mate.

My magic flared, flowing through me, adjusting my body to accept what my mate was giving me. The screw-like spiral of his dino-dick thrust in. It twisted in my wet heat as Zon jerked the chains that held me suspended to plunge deeper.

Zon was snarling and growling, his movements growing harsher with each thrust. I was probably going to have the imprint of the links in my skin permanently after this, but it was a small price to pay for quite possibly the best sex of my life.

With each stroke, Zon's length teased and stroked every hidden, sensitive place inside me. Places that had only been stimulated when Rez had claimed me.

For the first time, I found myself thankful for the chains supporting me. My breath was coming in quick pants, and my vision had grown fuzzy around the edges.

Be gentle. Injure my mate, and I will make you extinct—again, Rez snarled through the mind link.

She's mine too, Zon hissed back. His words were garbled and not quite human, but I was relieved to know he was still there.

"Zon?" I gasped between his brutal thrusts. "I love you. I'm proud to be your mate."

My raptor mate dropped his mouth to the skin between my neck and my shoulder. He gently nipped the skin between his teeth, preparing to mark me.

"I love you, my mate," Zon said out loud, his hoarse voice slightly more recognizable.

Reaching behind me, I pressed my hand to his neck. Releasing my magic, I let it flow between us, marking the raptor shifter as mine. Forever.

Sheathing himself inside me one final time, Zon roared his release. As his erection jerked inside me, it began to swell, locking us together. Scorching heat sizzled through me. The warmth combined with his ribbed monster cock gently pulsing against my most sensitive areas pushed me over the edge, as a mind-shattering orgasm robbed me of all thought, leaving me with only overwhelming sensation.

As we fought to catch our breath, my power hummed lazily around us, rippling across our skin.

I'd claimed Zon as my mate, and he'd claimed me as his.

With our bodies locked together, Zonkut gently freed me from the chains and lifted me in his arms. Settling himself on the floor, he cradled me against his chest. I twisted my torso to meet his eyes and was relieved to see the rounded human pupils that belonged solely to Zon.

"Just give me a few minutes to finish regaining control." His voice was rough with exhaustion.

Content that he would be okay, I relaxed against Zon's chest, letting myself enjoy the comforting heat of his body.

CHAPTER FIVE
-REZ-

What do you call a slutty brontosaurus?
A DINO-WHORE.

I watched as Zonkut held our little mate, his muscles relaxing as he regained control. The raptor shifter had thankfully calmed. With Zon no longer ready to tear into anything standing between him and his mate, I carefully lowered Jack to the ground.

Jack straightened his stretched-out shirt and nodded his head up at me in thanks. I had to hand it to the human. For the most part, he was taking life with us in stride. This couldn't be the life he had envisioned living, but he didn't complain. Arizona had done well when she claimed him.

My muscles quivered as the beast inside me pushed against the restraints holding him back. I was relieved Zonkut was no longer a danger to himself and others, but I was reaching my own breaking point.

Arizona's seductive magic was heavy in the air, brushing against my scales like a lover's kiss. After the whirlwind of heightened emotions I'd gone through during the dinner, I was struggling to remain in control. Only my friendship with Zonkut had kept me from killing the smaller dinosaur who dared touch my mate. I needed her, too.

With the scent of sex filling my lungs and her intoxicating magic soaking into my skin, I was fighting a losing war against instinct. Seeing the dark smudges of exhaustion under her eyes caused my heart to ache, and I continued to struggle against the other side of my nature.

Zonkut had kept himself from injuring her, but he hadn't been gentle. How could I ask her to calm my inner beast with the reassurance of her touch when her body required time to rest and recover?

I blew out a frustrated sigh.

"You know she will be upset when she finds out you needed help but didn't ask her," Jack whispered.

Snorting, I snapped my teeth at the impertinent human male who was brave enough—or stupid enough—to tell me what I should do.

"Hey, man! Don't eat the messenger." Jack lifted his hands in surrender. "I'm just saying you should trust your mate. We're her perfect match, right? Which means we were made for her. She can handle whatever you throw at her. Trust her."

He was right. Exhaustion weighed heavily on me, and

my head drooped. I should be honest with her and tell her I wasn't doing as well as I'd led her to believe.

Jack's lips curved into a smirk. "Maybe you could figure out how to shift back first, though? She can handle a lot, but this might be too much."

Didn't he think I would if I could? It was all I could do to hold on to a shred of my human mind with my tyrannosaurus side fighting against me. But Jack was right. I had to shift back, because until I did, there was no way to find the comfort and reassurance I needed from my mate.

It was unfortunate I was the largest living dinosaur on Earth. As an alpha, I'd had the power to force Zonkut's shift. I'd pushed his beast back just enough to allow Zonkut to regain some level of control. It would have been helpful if someone could do the same for me.

Unable to shift, but unable to be away from my mate's touch for another minute, I made my way to her side with heavy steps. Lowering myself to the concrete floor, I dropped my head and pressed my nose against my mate's back.

"Rez," Arizona whispered, reaching out a hand to stroke my scales.

Her heavy-lidded eyes shone with happiness. Glancing at Zonkut's face, I found it more relaxed than I'd seen in many years.

He looked happy.

Well, that made one of us.

Arizona's bare thighs lay across Zon's lap, her dress still bunched around her waist. I knew I shouldn't, but the temptation to taste her was too strong. Flicking out the tip of my tongue, I licked her.

With a tyrannosaurus-sized tongue, just the tip of it covered her entire leg—from ankle to hip. Her sweet skin tasted of heaven and her unique magic. It was too much, and my eyes rolled to the back of my head.

"Ew. That's weird, Rez." Arizona shivered.

Even though she pretended to be disgusted, there was no mistaking the way her magic crackled or the heat in her gaze.

You taste good enough to eat, I whispered through the bond.

Arizona's laugh was music to my ears. "Rez, that would be sexy... if you weren't a T-Rex who's fully capable of eating me in one bite."

White-hot pain sizzled along every nerve-ending in my body, and I swallowed a growl. It was becoming harder to breathe, and my desperate longing for my mate pounded like a drum through my skull.

Closing my eyes, I tried to focus my energy on maintaining at least a semblance of my humanity. The last thing this night needed was for my beast to take full control and allow all my primal instincts to take over.

"Are you okay?" Arizona's hands stroked my cheek.

There was a whisper of fabric, and I cracked open my eye to find her crawling off Zon's lap. Arizona hugged my snout, pressing her cheek against the top of my muzzle.

I need you, my queen.

Arizona tilted her head to study my open eye. "Then shift back and take me."

Her husky purr was nearly my undoing. I squeezed my eye closed again, as restraining my shifter side moved from simply challenging to agony.

"He can't." Zon must have realized the internal battle I was fighting and answered for me. "His beast is fighting him, and it is all Rezkac can do to keep the tyrannosaurus from taking over completely. Sadly, his beast won't back down until he is satisfied by mating you, but he can't mate with you until he's able to shift to his human form."

Arizona's breathing grew faster, and her fingers tightened on my scales.

"What can we do to help him?" Arizona's voice rose in panic. "We have to do something!"

"I'm not aware of a way to force him to shift other than having an alpha shifter command it. And there are none alive who are large enough, or powerful enough, to force a beast like his to back down."

I was thankful Zonkut was answering her questions, as it allowed me to use my waning energy on my internal struggle.

There was a long silence, then Ari spoke, her voice hesitant. "Maybe I could do it?"

Zonkut's sharp bark of laughter echoed around the warehouse, and I couldn't help but give a small snort of surprise as well.

Opening my eyes, I found my little mate scowling at me. "You two don't think I can?"

"Babe, Rezkac is the alpha among shifters. His beast takes commands from no one… especially not a human."

Stubbornly, Ari lifted her chin. "I'm not fully human, though. I'm part Vazi."

Zonkut's eyebrows rose. "You are only part Vazi, and while your magic is strong, you have no idea how to control it. What if you send your magic surging into him, and it just makes his beast stronger and more out of control?"

Zon's concerns were valid, but our mate was not to be dissuaded. "I might not know exactly how my magic works, but it seems to respond to what I ask of it. This could work. Besides, what other choice do we have?"

I shot a look at Zon, not surprised to find my own frustration mirrored in his expression. We both knew there wasn't another option. I could continue to fight my beast and hope he gave in before I did. But that was a risk, too, especially with the exhaustion I was already feeling. If I passed out before getting the beast to give in, he would take control.

Rez, do you want me to try? Ari's words drifted through the link.

I was terrified of what might go wrong, but was too tired to keep struggling.

Giving in, I whispered a single word into the bond. *Yes.*

Arizona took a deep breath, pressing her palms flat against my scales. For a moment, nothing happened. Then warmth began to ripple from her hands, and the scent of her magic grew stronger until it was the only scent in the warehouse.

The tendrils of her delicious magic spread through me, touching every cell in my body until I vibrated with her power.

Shift. Arizona pressed the command into my mind.

My beast paused for a moment, intrigued by our mate. I tried to shift, but instincts still drove my beast, and he wasn't relinquishing control of our form.

Ari's huff of annoyance was adorable. She stuck out the tip of her tongue, and her brow creased as her concentration deepened. If I'd been in my human form, I would have sucked the tip of her tongue into my mouth and followed up by kissing the very breath from her lungs.

The sweet scent of her magic took on a toasted caramel scent as the heat of her magic turned from warm to scorching.

SHIFT, Arizona growled into the bond.

Every fiber of my being focused on our mate, temporarily halting our struggle for full dominance.

Still, my beast refused to back down.

Once those primal instincts of protecting our mate kicked in, it was impossible to turn them off until the beast was convinced our mate was satisfied with our worthiness as a mate.

"Stubborn man—er, dino... shifter... whatever!" Arizona groaned in frustration.

Zon rested his hands on her shoulders, gently trying to pull her away. "Sweetheart, this isn't going to work. I've never heard of even a full Vazi being able to give an order to an alpha male tyrannosaurus. Rez's beast is too strong for him to restrain. How do you think you will control him?"

"I'm not every other Vazi." Ari's eyelids snapped open, and I caught my breath. Her beautiful gray eyes glowed and sparkled. "And I'm not finished yet."

The walls of the room contracted as she sucked in a deep breath, readying herself for whatever she had planned. Ari's hair lifted from her shoulders as though electricity were in the air and lightning was going to strike nearby at any moment. A streak of pink magic flicked across her skin, and then another.

"What the he—" Jack shouted from somewhere behind me.

Uh, Rezkac? She isn't supposed to be this strong. Zon's worry seeped into my mind.

Maybe you should stop underestimating me, Arizona growled, somehow breaking into the private link I shared with Zonkut.

I didn't get a chance to answer before she blasted her magic into me.

"I said shift, and I meant it!" Arizona screamed, her determined gaze locked with mine.

My bellow of pain threatened to bring down the warehouse on top of us as liquid fire seemed to replace the very blood in my veins. Every muscle and bone in my massive body turned to jelly as Arizona's power rearranged the shifter magic in my DNA. She gave the beast inside me no choice but to relinquish control as our mate forcefully activated the human form, and temporarily turned off the shifter magic.

"SHIFT!" my mate commanded a final time, and to my utter shock, my beast bowed to her.

The air shimmered, humming like angry bees, as my body shifted to my human form. With a strangled groan, I collapsed. The cool concrete was a relief against my burning skin, and I closed my aching eyes.

"It worked," Zonkut whispered in shock.

"Of course it did." Ari tried to sound confident, but her nervous giggle gave away the fact she'd surprised herself.

"Our queen can do anything," I murmured, too exhausted to even open my eyes.

Cool air blew across my skin, followed by the press of Arizona's soft lips against my cheek. "I'm sorry if I hurt you."

"I'm fine... just need a minute to catch my breath," I croaked, the exhaustion in my voice contradicting my words.

In truth, it felt as though I'd just trekked through the heart of a volcano. My body quivered, jerking from aftershocks caused by her magic. I needed to sleep for a week, and even that might not be long enough to recover from the inner turmoil stirred by both my beast and her power.

"Zon? Can you teleport us to the hotel? We are a mess, and I don't want to risk catching the attention of a taxi driver," Arizona asked.

I cracked open one eyelid to find Arizona chewing on

her thumbnail, anxiously glancing between Zonkut and myself.

"Babe, I am so high on your magic right now, I could probably teleport us around the world several times without feeling a strain." Zon chuckled. "Although Jack isn't going to like the way it feels."

"How about I call a ride and catch up with you guys? I'll bring Albert with me." Jack suggested, the tapping of his fingers on the glass telling me he was already using his phone to order a ride.

"Whatever floats your ship, bro." Zonkut shrugged.

"Boat," Arizona corrected automatically. "It's 'whatever floats your boat.'"

Zon ignored her. Reaching forward, he wrapped one arm around her waist. "Let's go."

My skull pounded as though a pterodactyl was trying to crack it open, and my muscles burned as though I'd torn every single one of them. Even the roots of my hair ached. In summary, I felt like a steaming pile of dino dung.

When Zon grabbed my wrist, and the world began to fade away, I welcomed the temporary bliss of nothingness with open arms.

CHAPTER SIX
-ARIZONA-

Which dinosaur knew the most words?
THE THESAURUS!

We materialized in the comfortable two-room suite that had been arranged for us by the museum. I'd explained to Teresa that I was bringing my two assistants—a.k.a. Rez and Zon—and a suite would allow for better team planning.

In reality, Albert had enjoyed being able to stretch out in one of the empty twin beds in the second room. This left the guys and me to pile into the king-sized bed in the larger room.

"Ugh. I'll never get used to that." I clutched my stomach and breathed through my nose, trying to settle the nausea teleporting always caused.

Rez sank to the floor with a hard thud.

I rushed to his side, stroking the sweaty strands of black hair from his face. "Rez!"

I'm fine. Stop worrying, my love, Rez whispered into my mind.

"Zon, help me get Rez into the bed." If we could get him in bed, he could get some much-needed rest.

"Not with the way he smells." Zon wrinkled his nose. "If we're sharing a bed, then all of us need to clean up first. Give me a minute."

Zon disappeared into the bathroom, and a few seconds later, I heard water splash into the oversized tub.

Tired as I was, Zon had a point. I was covered in dirt and grime from the chains and the concrete floor. It would feel good to be clean before crawling between the pristine white hotel sheets.

Returning to the bedroom, Zon walked by Rez and scooped me into his arms.

"What are you doing? I can walk to the bathroom! I need you to help Rez!" My protests went unheeded.

"Babe, I finally got to claim you as my mate." Zon nuzzled my neck. "I promise I'll take care of Rez too, but you have to understand that all my beast and I care about right now is caring for you. You're our first priority."

My heart fluttered. In the chaos of defusing the situation with both my mates' shifter halves, Zon and I hadn't really been able to celebrate our bonding.

Once in the bathroom, Zon set me on my feet and quickly lifted the tattered dress over my head, letting it fall to the floor. Since the dress had a built-in bra, and he'd already torn away my underwear in the warehouse, I stood naked in front of him.

Zon caught my hand and guided me into the tub. With a sigh, I sank into the warm water. Placing a quick kiss on the top of my head, Zon stood, leaving me alone in the bathroom.

I ducked beneath the water, letting the stress of the day melt away. When I surfaced, Zon had returned to the bathroom. To my relief, Rez was standing but leaning heavily against Zon. Rez's intense stare was fixed on me.

Both my mates could shift between human and dino forms without destroying their clothing, but since neither man had been wearing clothes when they'd shifted to head for the museum, they were both currently in the buff.

It was a sight for my exhausted eyes… and other parts of my anatomy.

Pull yourself together. I gave myself a mental shake, barely resisting the urge to smack myself.

Zon and I had just had mind-blowing sex not even an hour ago, and here I was, already thinking about sex again. Maybe it was becoming an addiction. Maybe I needed to go on a no-sex detox or something?

"NO!" both Rez and Zon roared in unison.

"Quit listening to my private conversations. It could be a serious problem…" I dipped a little deeper beneath the water to hide my flushed cheeks.

"It is not a problem. This is natural. Your body is using sex to siphon off the excess magic you aren't able to handle." Zon rushed to nip my line of questioning off.

"Plus, it wouldn't surprise me if your magic is adjusting your libido to match ours. Shifters are more in touch with their primal needs." His wink had my stomach dancing an Irish jig.

Was that good news for me, or bad? I opened my mouth to ask, then changed my mind and closed it.

With help, Rez stepped into the bath. He sank down beside me, body stiff and chest rumbling with a groan.

My heart twisted. "I did hurt you, didn't I?"

Scooting closer to him, I brushed my fingers across his stubbled jaw.

"I'm fine, my queen." Rez caught my hand and pressed a gentle kiss to my palm. "You did an incredible thing tonight. I would be in much worse condition if you didn't force my shift."

He gave me a sleepy smile, his eyelids drooping and reminding me of why we were in the tub.

"Let's get you cleaned up so we can all get some sleep." I grabbed a rag from the basket on the edge of the tub, soaped it up, and began to wash the grime from Rez's skin.

Without saying a word, Zon kneeled by the tub. Grabbing one of the hotel's tiny shampoo bottles, he squeezed some in his hand, and with a tenderness that surprised me, started massaging my scalp.

"Zon, I can wash myself," I protested, but he continued working the shampoo through my long hair.

"Let me care for you." Leaning in, Zon kissed my cheek. "I enjoy it."

And so, while I washed Rez, Zon continued to wash

the dirt and grime from my skin. It was a strange combination. Sensual, but at the same time comforting. Had we not been so tired, it probably would have led to something more.

Zon had just deposited me on the bed and was helping Rez when Jack pushed open the hotel room door. Under one arm, he held Albert's pet carrier, and under the other, was a brown paper bag.

"Albert and I figured we all needed something to eat, so we stopped by the Chinese restaurant down the block." Jack sat the food on the tiny dinette table. "Let me settle Albert in the other room, and I'll dish it up."

I was relieved that at least one of my mates seemed to like the little ham.

Rez scooted into bed beside me, tucking me under his arm. "Mmm. Hey there, beautiful."

"Maybe you should wait until you get some stamina back before you start flirting?" Zon chuckled, shaking his head. "I'm going to go take a quick shower."

The next hour was spent in companionable silence as we all stuffed our faces with orange chicken, fried rice, Kung Pao Chicken, and scallion pancakes. When Jack's cell phone rang, I jumped in fright, nearly tossing my plate into Rez's lap.

Jack checked the screen. "It's Teresa."

My stomach pitched uncomfortably. I wanted to tell him to let it go to voicemail, but I had to face her eventually. Better to answer now than open the door to police officers… again.

Although, looking at my handsome detective, I had to admit that situation had worked out nicely.

"I'll answer it." Sliding the green dot on the screen, I clicked on the speaker and said, "Hello?"

"Hi, Arizona! This is Teresa." The curator sounded out of breath, but not angry, which I hoped was a good sign.

She didn't give me time to respond, which was just as well since I didn't know how best to plead my case. "Listen, the last of the guests just left the museum, and let me tell you"—she paused to catch her breath—"everyone thought you were incredible! The evening was a success!"

"It… It was?" I stammered, sure I'd heard incorrectly.

"Yes!" Teresa's excitement was palpable even through the phone. "While you didn't run the dinosaur rampage concept by me, and I'm not sure you even planned it ahead of time, the patrons loved getting to experience a scene straight from a movie set."

She'd given me an out, and I wasn't about to admit it hadn't been part of a genius mastermind plan. "That's great?"

"Arizona, the donations poured in after you left. We raised more tonight than we've raised over the past year. I couldn't be happier. Well, I'd be happier if I didn't have a destroyed lawn that needed to be cleaned, but I'll have that fixed tomorrow."

"My team and I are happy to come clean up in the morning," I offered, hoping to stay in Teresa's good graces and honestly feeling bad for the mess we'd left.

"*Psh*. Don't worry about it. We have amazing staff.

However, there is something you could do for me." Teresa had gotten around to the point of her call.

"Yes?" I asked, not sure where this was going.

"One of our biggest benefactors has made us an incredible offer, but it involves you. Would you be willing to stop by in the morning and look it over?"

What I really wanted was to head home with Albert Einswine and my mates, but I also wanted to keep Teresa happy… so I agreed.

We created a plan for the following morning, and I ended the call a few minutes later. Feeling relieved Teresa didn't seem upset, I finished the last of my food before snuggling between Rez and Jack. Zon stretched across the foot of the bed, his hands massaging my calves.

After the insanely long day we'd just survived, sleep claimed us quickly.

CHAPTER SEVEN
-ARIZONA-

Why do museums exhibit old dinosaur bones?
BECAUSE THEY CAN'T AFFORD NEW ONES!

I gripped Albert's leash a little tighter and took a steadying breath to calm my nerves. Reaching out, I swung open the heavy glass door and stepped inside the museum's interior. The sweat trickling down my spine from the Texas heat chilled at the blast of air-conditioning, causing a wave of goosebumps to travel across my skin.

Yep. It was absolutely the heat causing me to sweat, and had nothing to do with the fact I was about to face Teresa. Sure, she'd reassured me over the phone that everything was hunky-dory, but she could have just told me that to make sure I'd show up today without a fuss. For all I knew, she had cops waiting to arrest me in her office.

But did it really matter? There was no way I could go on

the run with two dinosaurs. If the museum planned to press charges, it was probably better to face the heat head-on.

When my eyes adjusted to the dim interior, and I saw the two men standing beside Teresa, I found myself wishing she'd invited the cops instead.

Bartholomew.

Albert gave a disgusted grunt that mirrored my own thoughts.

Kneeling to place a gentle pat on his head, I murmured under my breath, "Yeah. I feel the same way, buddy."

I was seriously considering turning on my heel and heading back the way I'd come when Teresa's attention locked onto me. "Arizona! We're so thrilled you could make time for us this morning."

Arranging my face into what was probably more grimace than a smile, I made my way to Teresa, with Albert trotting along beside me. "Good morning."

"You remember Bartholomew Burkhardt?" Teresa motioned to the man on her left before nodding at the man on her right. "And this is his accountant, Scott Center."

I took both men's offered hands with the same enthusiasm I would've had if I'd been shaking the sticky, snot-covered hand of one of the first graders on my museum tour.

Actually, I'd have preferred the snot-covered hand.

Bartholomew held my hand a tad longer than I was comfortable with, and I found myself wishing Jack had come with me. Albert's high-pitched squeal made the man jerk, and he yanked his hand away from me.

"What in the blue blazes?!" Bart's wild-eyed gaze landed on the pint-sized porker at my side. "What is that creature doing here?"

"My apologies for not warning you! Arizona was unable to leave him unattended in the hotel room, and her partner, Jack, was busy with software updates on the dino models. I told her it would be fine to bring him with her as long as he stayed leashed," Teresa rushed to explain.

When I'd given her the lame excuse about Jack needing to focus, I'd expected to get into some argument, but she'd readily agreed that I could bring my pet.

That wasn't the real reason I hadn't wanted to leave Albert, though. I wanted Jack to stay and guard my dino mates. And with both shifters still on edge from the night before, having Albert hanging around wasn't likely to help with calming their nerves.

There was a second reason I'd wanted Jack to stay with Rez and Zon, a far more worrisome reason. I didn't trust that someone—like Bartholomew—wouldn't send spies to skulk around the warehouse.

This whole morning meeting might be a setup to lure me away from my 'prop dinosaurs' so a competitor could send in their guys to study my 'technology.'

Rez tried to reassure me he could easily eat anyone who learned too much. But I'd made it abundantly clear that if he wanted to keep kissing me, he'd better keep humans off his food chain.

"I see," Bartholomew said curtly.

Scott kneeled beside Albert, reaching out to pet him. At

the twinkle in Albert's eyes, my heart lurched. Tilting my head down so my hair created a curtain, blocking anyone from seeing my lips, I mouthed 'behave' to the pig.

Then I remembered he couldn't understand English beyond the words 'walk,' 'treat,' and 'good boy'… At least, I didn't think he could.

My doubts regarding his level of comprehension were further reinforced when my piglet sighed and rolled his eyes. Pigs didn't roll their eyes, did they?

To my relief, Albert Einswine behaved.

Scott gave Albert one last pat and stood. "It's rare to meet anyone who owns a pig as a pet. I've read they are incredibly intelligent."

"Yes, it's creepy how smart he is." I side-eyed the pig, who looked up at me with a wide-eyed innocence I wasn't falling for.

While I didn't believe he was a demon like Rez and Zon claimed, I no longer believed he was a well-behaved piglet, either.

"Should we walk around and take a quick look at some of the newer exhibits?" Teresa suggested.

"Of course, lead the way." Scott gave her a wide grin and stepped to the side, allowing me to walk in front of him and Bartholomew as we followed Teresa down a long hall.

Hurrying to catch up with her, I whispered, "I thought we were meeting to go over a proposal you received last night?"

"We are! Bartholomew just wanted to be here when I presented it to you, so he could help answer any questions." Teresa squeezed my arm, her excitement bubbling over.

My stomach turned to lead and sank to the floor. I didn't want any part of whatever Bartholomew planned to offer, but after the fundraising dinner fiasco, I couldn't exactly tell Teresa that.

Swallowing back my frustration at being forced to spend time in Bart's company, I resigned myself to enduring the meeting. I really wished my guys were here with me as backup.

Albert's cold nose pressed against my ankle. It was a sweet reminder I wasn't completely alone. Scooping him into my arms, I cuddled him against my chest. A pet potbelly might not truly count as backup, but his presence did wonders to calm my nerves.

"I'm glad you're here," I whispered against his velvety ear.

Albert snorted in response and relaxed in my arms as I followed Teresa. She gave us an impromptu tour of the museum, and despite my misgivings, I found myself drawn into her descriptions of each exhibit.

This museum was at least twice the size of the museum I'd worked at. Most of the pieces in these exhibits were far more valuable than anything my museum had been able to acquire. I had to hand it to her, Teresa was an incredible museum curator, and it was obvious she took great pride in her work.

About thirty minutes into the tour, Bart looked at his watch and cleared his throat. "As much as I have enjoyed seeing what my money has been used for, I have a meeting in an hour. How about we head to your office and discuss the proposal?"

Teresa quickly hid her disappointment at the tour being cut short. "Yes, of course! We certainly don't want to keep you from your busy schedule. Follow me, please."

It was a short walk to her office, and as we entered, Teresa paused at her assistant's desk. "Cathy, would you mind bringing refreshments for my guests into the office?"

With a cheerful smile, her assistant pushed away from the desk and headed toward a tiny kitchen. Teresa continued into her office, and following behind her, I stumbled to a stop as I crossed the threshold. My entire focus was drawn to the room's floor-to-ceiling bookshelves filled with collectibles.

It was exactly the type of office I'd expect from a broody Egyptology professor. Historians and movie set designers alike would drool over her study. Every book, artifact, and antique treasure was perfectly displayed and arranged among similar treasures.

It was the kind of place I didn't want to hang out in too long for fear I'd sneeze and knock everything off the shelves. I was the human equivalent of a bull in a china shop, or a kangaroo in a glass museum.

Worse, what if I accidentally bumped into a dinosaur shifter bone and magically brought them back to life in here?

Don't look directly at any of the bones. Don't do it, Ari. I chanted the words in my mind like a mantra.

Since I still wasn't one hundred percent clear about how the magic that brought Rez and Zon back to life worked, I had no way of knowing how to wake up any other dinosaurs—or, more accurately, how to prevent that from happening.

We had enough to deal with, so I'd carefully avoided looking directly at any of the museum's dinosaur bone collection since our arrival, and I planned to keep it up. It was probable that I needed to touch the bones, but I wasn't taking chances at this point. It was like that old saying; better safe than sorry when it came to sex and dinosaur bones.

Why couldn't my many-many-greats-ago-grandma have just left me cute things she knitted like other grandmas? Nope, mine had to leave me freaking dinosaur shifters.

"Here, Arizona. Take the seat nearest me, so you can see the paperwork too." Teresa tapped the back of a plush leather seat that was pushed slightly to the side of her desk.

Bartholomew and Scott settled into two high-back leather chairs. Not wasting any time, Bartholomew pulled a sheet of paper from his coat pocket and handed it to Teresa.

"This is my proposal. As soon as we can come to an agreement, Scott will write you the check." Crossing his arms over his chest, Bart leaned back against his chair.

Cathy slipped into the room, setting a tray with a pitcher of water and several sparkling glasses on the sideboard. After pouring us each a glass, she quietly excused herself.

When we were alone again, Teresa slid on a pair of

glasses and unfolded the paper. My gaze darted between her and Bartholomew, trying to piece together what type of proposal the arrogant douche had conjured that could involve the museum and me.

I didn't have to wait long for my answer.

Teresa flattened the paper on the glossy surface of her desk. "I spoke with the museum board this morning, and we are in awe of your generosity."

An awkward pause followed, and I decided it was time for me to speak up. Clearing my throat, I asked, "I think I've missed something. I'm not really sure why I am here?"

With a chuckle, Teresa slid the glasses from her face. "Oh, yes. That would be important information to share with you, wouldn't it?"

I gave a weak laugh, trying to cling to positivity but feeling more anxious with each passing minute I spent in Bartholomew's company. I wanted nothing to do with him, but I also wanted to stay on the museum's good side.

Wary, I eyed Teresa as my anxiety started getting the best of me. I caught myself unconsciously rubbing Albert's velvety ear between my fingers. It was ridiculous how calming the motion was, and once again, I was relieved my tiny pet was with me.

"You are a pivotal part of this, my dear." Teresa smiled, her eyes sparkling as she slid the paper across the desk toward me. "Here, why don't you read it for yourself, and then we can answer any questions you may have."

Reaching out, I hesitantly took the paper. Already suspecting I wasn't going to like whatever it said, I began to read. It seemed that Barty-Boy's company was loaded, and he was interested in sponsoring a week-long summer camp aimed at getting children interested in paleontology, and by extension, preserving history through museums.

On paper, the proposed program sounded amazing. It was overly generous for everyone involved. If it hadn't been for his utter lack of respecting my boundaries the previous evening, I would've been absolutely wowed by his generosity and benevolence.

Teresa might be fooled, but I most certainly was not.

According to the proposal, Bartholomew wanted to donate a generous seven-figure sum to create a dinosaur zoological area on the museum grounds. Everything would have to be done quickly since school would let out in a week, and Bartholomew wanted to run the summer camp a week later.

The donation would cover the cost of a team of groundskeepers, all necessary landscaping needs, advertising for the new program, child-friendly booklets, and art supplies, and an audio team to create sound effects that would play through the speaker system hidden throughout the garden.

Last, it would cover a generous salary for my team, and dinosaur prototypes, to work the dinosaur exhibits through the summer.

This wasn't the type of salary a museum paid a cleaner, either. This was the type of payout you hoped to earn after going to college for a decade.

With my current situation, it would certainly help things

out. Jack claimed he was more than able to support us, and Rez had assured me they just had to locate some of their buried assets, and finances wouldn't ever be an issue for us.

But I was a strong, independent woman who was used to providing for herself and earning a paycheck. I didn't quite trust the dinos to remember where they had left their treasures. For all we know, their various stashes may have already been discovered over the past thousands of years.

I chewed on my lip and stroked Albert's ear as I contemplated the offer.

There was no doubt in my mind that this was Bart's way of keeping my dinosaurs in town. Bartholomew probably wanted more time so he could either bully me into creating an agreement with his company to use our technology, or so he could have his team study the dinosaurs closer.

The amount of money he was willing to spend to get that opportunity made it crystal clear he was practically salivating over the possibility of stealing our tech... or trying to.

It was kind of hard to steal technology that didn't exist. But there was no way I would reveal that juicy tidbit.

I couldn't, not if I wanted to keep my shifters safe.

But would it be stupid to turn down this kind of salary? Just because I didn't trust the guy? I wasn't sure.

"What do you think, Arizona?" Teresa asked, picking up the paper I'd laid back on her desk. "Do you think Dinovation would be willing to loan their dinosaurs to the museum for a week-long contract?"

"Um." I tried to find the right words. "I'm really not sure they can allow that with our deadlines on other projects," I hedged, not wanting to be hasty and make a decision I'd regret. "I can speak with Dinovation. Even if they're willing, I know they'll have restrictions and requirements that would need to be met."

"Absolutely! And I am sure we would be more than able to cater to those requirements." Teresa rushed to assure me.

"Would there be security measures to prevent visitors from touching the dinosaurs? As we talked about prior to the dinner event, Dinovation doesn't want anyone touching the dinosaurs. Not staff, and definitely not visitors. This is a condition they will not be willing to bend on." I couldn't help but study Bartholomew as I gave the condition, but his only reaction was a slight twitch in his left eye.

"That is understandable. We wouldn't want the dinosaurs to be damaged, or the gardens to be trampled. There would be fencing around each dinosaur's exhibit. It will add to the feel of a zoo with live animals, or dinosaurs, which I believe our guests will love." Teresa eagerly jotted notes on a pad of paper.

"We would need an answer fairly quickly, though. We don't have much time to prepare the exhibits and start the advertising. Our team will have to work overtime to even make this happen." Teresa looked over the rim of her glasses at me. "How long do you think it will take for Dinovation to come to a decision?"

"I'm sure a quick decision can be made. Although, I can't guarantee it will be the one you are hoping for."

Albert squirmed on my lap, drawing my attention away from the curator as I tried to calm him down.

"We understand. Do you think you could speak with them and give us at least a list of some of their requirements? That way, our team can address any concerns," Scott asked, sitting back in his chair and resting one ankle across his leg.

"Better yet, do you have a number where we can speak to the CEO of Dinovation directly? Perhaps that would be easier for negotiations." Bartholomew, ever devious, prodded for more information about the mysterious company.

"I'm not at liberty to give out that information." Setting my jaw, I prepared for him to argue, but something in my gaze must have warned him I wasn't going to budge on this point.

Smart man.

Not really.

"Well, then. Let me make our intentions clear, and you can relay the information to your boss." Bartholomew smirked when he said *boss*, and pulled out a second piece of paper from his breast coat pocket. "Here is a copy of the offer presented to the museum, as well as a second page that covers the benefits and payment that will be made to Dinovation and whomever they choose to staff the exhibits —should they agree to partner with us on this project."

Standing, Bartholomew turned to Teresa. "Our offer is open for the next three days. After that, we will look into other donation opportunities… elsewhere. I'd really hate to do that since I have enjoyed working with this museum. I remember being enthralled by dinosaurs as a kid, and my company would love to take it to the next level for kids through this camp."

Smooth. He'd delivered the threat of taking away his backing of the museum, all the while wrapping it in a poignant childhood memory that was sure to pull at the heartstrings.

I might love to shop, but I wasn't buying his bullcrap.

Teresa stood and held out her hand. "We understand it is a time-sensitive offer, and I'm sure we are all eager to get everything settled quickly. Thank you again for proposing this magnificent opportunity."

Scott stood as well and, turning to me, held out his hand. "It was a pleasure, Ms. Charcoal."

Releasing my hold on Albert's leash, I shook Scott's hand. It wasn't his fault his boss was an arrogant jerkwad.

Albert saw an opportunity and took full advantage of it.

CHAPTER EIGHT
-ARIZONA-

Where did the dinosaur clown get a job?
AT THE CARNIVORE.

Leaping from my lap, Albert darted between Scott's legs. He launched himself at Bart's expensive-looking loafers.

"Albert, no! Come back!" I screamed.

But did the four-legged salami care what I wanted?

Absolutely not.

With an oink of unbridled glee, Albert Einswine bit down hard on the soft leather tassels. A single hard yank of his head was all it took for Albert to detach the leather dangling bits. He tossed them to the ornate Persian rug while I looked on in utter horror.

I bet money those tassels cost more than I made in a week of cleaning and giving tours.

"I'm so sorry!" I apologized, lunging toward Albert's curly-tailed backside.

Bartholomew's face had turned the color of a ripe plum, but to his credit, when he spoke, his voice was even. "Don't worry about it. This was an old pair of shoes."

I doubted Bart was telling the truth. He wasn't going to risk upsetting me while he still wanted me to make this deal happen.

"I'll talk to my team tonight!" I shouted as I rushed past him, through the door, and into the outer office area.

Running past Cathy's empty desk, I closed the distance between the potbelly pig and myself. But just as I got near enough to snatch him, Cathy swung open the main door.

Albert didn't think twice before darting through her legs and out the door. My blood turned to ice as I watched him scamper into the main hall that trailed through the museum.

The next fifteen minutes were spent chasing Albert as he dodged between visitors' legs, trash cans, strollers, and various oversized plants. To my unending embarrassment, Teresa and two security officers had joined in the hunt.

Albert seemed to have captured the energy of a battery-powered pink bunny, and he had me chasing his jiggly buttcheeks from one room to the other.

Was there some type of pig agility event like they held for dogs? If so, I needed to enter Albert, because he was sure to win.

I lost sight of him as he disappeared into the gift shop.

By the time I made it to the shop entry, I was huffing and puffing hard enough to blow my little pig's house down.

Entering the shop, I came face-to-face with a hulking security guard who was holding a squirming Albert in his hands. Teresa stepped out from behind the guard. She was out of breath and laughing.

"I thought we might be able to cut him off if we came this way, and it worked! I had no idea pigs were so fast!" she wheezed, eyes twinkling.

"Yeah, me neither." I took Albert from the guard's arms, wincing at the pain in my side from our impromptu sprint. "Thank you for catching him. I promise he's normally a lot better behaved."

Teresa waved away my frustration. "No harm was done, and I think the visitors got a kick out of a free show. Besides, I could use a bit more exercise."

I wondered if she was so chill because she was hoping I'd get Dinovation to agree to the summer camp, or if she was really just this nice.

"I guess I better get going. I'd like to go ahead and talk to the bosses at Dinovation this afternoon and get their thoughts on the proposal." Deciding it was best not to push my luck, I began edging toward the door, but stopped when I glanced down at Albert. "What's that?"

Teresa stepped forward, taking the object from Albert's jaws. "Let's see what you have there, cutie."

Turning it in her hand, Teresa inspected the item before showing me.

"A dinosaur bone? When did he manage to snatch that?" I exclaimed, my mouth going dry.

"It's just a toy. Albert wanted to pick out a gift from the gift shop before you two left," Teresa chuckled, holding the bone back out to Albert, who carefully took it in his tiny jaws.

"Oh no! Let me grab my wallet—" I began, only to be cut off by Teresa.

"Pish posh! Let him have a souvenir from his visit. These replicas are less than $5 a piece, so it is honestly not a big deal. Now, shoo! The sooner you leave, the sooner we will hopefully be able to get started." She rubbed her hands together in glee, and I couldn't help but smile at her enthusiasm.

I'd love to work with her on this project, but only if the guys thought it was a good idea and that we could keep them safe… and far from Bartholomew's clutches.

CHAPTER NINE
-ARIZONA-

Why can't you hear a pterodactyl
when it goes to the toilet?
BECAUSE THE 'P' IS SILENT!

"Honeys, I'm home!" I called out as I entered the warehouse.

Sitting Albert Einswine down on the concrete floor, I grinned, watching him prance off toward the back of the building where we'd put a spare dog bed and an extra set of food bowls.

I shook my head at the dino bone toy still held proudly in his mouth. There was no doubt in my mind that I'd won the lottery when it came to oddball pet pigs.

Turning away from Albert, I searched the area for my men. "Guys?"

A frustrated groan drew my attention to the storage area near the back of the warehouse, and I hurried to see what was going on. I stopped at the doorway and had to bite back a laugh.

Rez, Zon and Jack were seated around a wobbly, metal worktable that had definitely seen better days. Cards were scattered on the battered, makeshift card table.

Snarling in annoyance, Zon dropped his head, letting it bang against the table. Rez was a little more restrained, and simply laid his handful of cards on the table, growling ancient curses under his breath.

"I take it the game isn't going well?" I asked with a giggle.

Jack shot me a wink. "It's going great for me."

Zon's head popped up, and the moment his gaze landed on me, he was out of his chair. He closed the distance between us in less time than it took for me to blink, and lifted me into his arms.

"Zon!" I squeaked in surprise, wrapping my legs around his waist to steady myself.

"I missed you, my love." His hot breath tickled against my neck as he pressed his mouth to my skin. "Also, this game is stupid." He added in a low growl.

"I missed you, too." It was all I could do to keep from moaning.

The way my body responded to my fated mates, was no joke. It was incredible, and highly addictive.

"He's just salty that I beat him again." Jack laughed, his chair scraping against the floor as he pushed away from the table.

Coming to stand behind us, Jack pried me from Zon's

arms. "Back off, raptor-boy. I've been a patient man, but you can't keep hogging our girl."

Zon's eyes flashed, a brilliant glow flaring in their depths. For a moment, I thought he was going to protest... or worse, start a fight.

Rez released a low trill, and I didn't need a translator to recognize it as a warning. Zon understood it as well. With an annoyed sigh, he allowed Jack to pull me into his arms.

I shouldn't love being passed around like a toy, but these men were my soulmates. Heck, if the chaos of every-day-life wasn't in the way, I'd enjoy spending the rest of my life being tossed between them like I was the lucky potato in a game of hot potato.

Sliding my arms around Jack's neck, I pressed my lips to his, savoring the way our lips melded together. Jack gripped my thighs, holding me against him as he returned to his seat. Sitting down, he settled me on his lap so that I straddled him.

A chair scraped loudly against the floor as Zon reclaimed his seat.

"How did it go? You seem anxious, but not upset." Rez asked.

I couldn't see his face since my back was to him, but I would bet all $109.06 in my checking account that his brow was wrinkled in concern. When Rez shifted, he was the most terrifying beast on earth, but underneath both his powerful forms, he was a gentle giant.

Girls dreamed of having a man who worried about their

heart and feelings... and my Rez took that tenderness to a Jurassic level.

Pulling my lips away from Jack's, I reassured him. "I'm fine, but we do have some things to talk about. Teresa needs an answer to her proposal ASAP."

"We'll do whatever you want," Zon answered immediately, as though that was the most logical response.

"Zon!" I chided between chuckles. "We are a family. *Partners.* That means we make decisions together on what will be best for our family."

With a bit of effort, I managed to turn myself around on Jack's lap so that I faced both Rez and Zon. Maybe without Jack's luscious, tempting lips so close to my face, I'd be able to focus better on the conversation we needed to have.

Condensing the morning's adventure at the museum, I tried to give the guys the most important pieces of information.

I glossed over how I'd felt when I realized Bartholomew was at the museum waiting for me along with Teresa. But nothing escaped my men's notice.

Zon's jaw tightened, and his eyes narrowed. Rez shifted in his seat, his irises darkening with rage. Jack wrapped his arms around my waist, pulling me tight against him.

"Did he touch you?" Zon asked, his voice rough with barely contained anger.

"No! Of course not! I don't think he's stupid enough to try something nefarious in a public place." I wasn't even sure I believed what I was saying.

"It is insane that Teresa allowed you two in the room together after what happened last night." Jack ground out.

"Honestly, his offer was just too good for her to resist." I blew out a tired sigh. "It's the type of offer any museum would be delighted to receive, so I can't really blame her for being willing to overlook last night's chaos."

"Why didn't you just leave?" Zon asked, "and tell them both to shove it?"

I chewed at my thumbnail. "Believe me, I wanted to! But I'm still worried that Theresa could change her mind about pressing charges for the damages done last night. That's a headache I really don't want to deal with- even if I could afford a ridiculously expensive attorney."

At the reminder of the damage their lack of control had caused, both shifters looked away. My heart ached. Rez and Zon were from a different time, and they were working overtime trying to get used to modern language and culture. And they had to do it while trying to maintain control of their beasts.

How could I ask them to be part of an exhibit for a week? They'd be stared at like animals stuck in a tiny zoo for hours on end. No way did I want to put my shifter mates through that stress. I refused to ask that of them.

Besides, there had to be some other way that I could help our family finances. I'd heard feet pictures were a hot commodity these days. I shuddered.

Leaning across the table, I grabbed one of each man's hands and gave them a little squeeze. "Never mind, it doesn't matter. It's too much to ask of you guys when you're still getting used to the world."

Rez lifted his eyes from studying the cards spread across the table. "You never ask too much of us. When we agreed to be bound to you as your mates, we were well aware of what we were getting ourselves into. We're supposed to make your life safer, easier, and more pleasurable- not make things harder on you."

"Stop that! You guys have made my life incredible since that very first night. Life isn't all sunshine and rainbows. Besides, how can we enjoy the happy highs in life, if we don't occasionally experience the lows? That's what shows us how much we have to be thankful for."

Pulling out my cell phone, I checked the time. "Hey, it's almost lunchtime. Did you guys have something in mind?" I tried to divert their attention with food.

It usually worked, but the men were laser-focused on what had happened at the museum.

"What are you thinking, Firefly?" Jack asked. "I may not be able to read your mind, but I was a decent detective, and you haven't told us everything." His hands slid up my back to massage my tense shoulders.

"Don't even worry about it. It's a bad idea, anyways. Food?" I asked again, still hoping to side-track their attention.

"She doesn't want to ask us." Rez provided helpfully.

"Stop reading my thoughts, Rez." I scrunched up my nose. "It's not fair."

"Is it because you don't trust us to help you, and maintain control of our dinosaur forms?" Zon raised a single eyebrow, "or is it because you are stubborn and unwilling to ask for help?"

"It's neither," Rez responded, not giving me a chance to reply, and ignoring the death glares I was shooting at him. "She's worried about us, and doesn't wish to stress us by asking for too much."

Zon snorted, "How is it asking too much for us to spend several hours a day in our dinosaur forms if it pleases you?" He honestly looked confused. "This provides a good cover story, doesn't it? The museum wishes to pretend we are real dinosaurs, which means they will keep other humans from touching us."

"Yes," I agreed reluctantly.

"It will help to raise awareness of dinosaurs in the young humans as well, which is something you seem to care about," Rez added.

I nodded my head in acknowledgment.

"Then, I fail to see the issue." Zon threw up his hands in exasperation.

Frustrated, I explained, "They're asking me to bring you guys each day to the museum, where you will be on display, so humans can gawk and photograph you guys. They're going to treat you like you're nothing more than animals."

Neither Zon nor Rez reacted. Both men studied my face, trying to puzzle out what my hang-up was.

Unable to hold it in, I blurted out, "It's degrading!"

Both men snorted.

"It might be degrading if we actually cared what they thought, Ari." Zon chuckled, amused by my outburst. "But we don't care. This allows you to maintain the illusion of independence by earning an income, which you seem to find some strange joy from. It achieves your goal of teaching humans about dinosaurs. Best of all, this gives us the freedom to release our beasts for several hours every day without concern of curious bystanders trying to touch us. The pros far outweigh the cons."

"They believe we are nothing more than intelligent machinery. Correct?" Rez asked.

"Yes," I confirmed.

"Then they are not purposefully degrading a living beast. I doubt Bartholomew's motives are pure, but I believe Teresa has good intentions." Rez finished.

Zon leaned back in his chair, crossing his arms over his broad muscled chest. "Besides, this really isn't much different than the mascots who show up at big events to interact with fans. They are humans dressed up as animals, who get paid to pretend to be the creature they are dressed as. The only difference is we are truly shifting into our dinosaur forms, while they are just pretending."

"I agree with Zonkut." Rez rubbed his jaw. "If you wish to do this, we'll support you. In fact, I believe it could be a good thing. I'd enjoy being able to shift more often, and I know my beast would too."

Craning my head around to see Jack's expression, I asked, "And you? What do you think, especially after last night?"

Jack shrugged. "As long as the right precautions are put into place, and they honor the boundaries we give them, I don't think it's a terrible idea. If the contract was for longer than a week, I'd be less eager to accept it. I say let's go for it!"

CHAPTER TEN
-ARIZONA-

What do you call a dinosaur who is a noisy sleeper?
A TYRANNO-SNORUS!

W e spent the next thirty minutes creating a list of requirements that would need to be included for us to sign the agreement.

Still perched on Jack's lap, I drummed my pen on the table. "Well, I guess that covers everything."

"It's about time. I still can't believe humans need words written on paper to remember their agreements." Rez stretched his arms above his head, his shirt riding up just enough to give me a nice peek at his abs.

Yummy. Was it snack time?

"You've done a good job. Now stop worrying. It will be fine." Jack hooked his chin over my shoulder so that our cheeks were pressed together.

I turned to give him a kiss, but Jack angled his face, so

my kiss landed on his lips instead of his jaw as I'd intended. Using it to his advantage, he nipped my lower lip between his teeth. The sparkle in his eyes promised naughty things, and my stomach quivered as a hot flush traveled across my skin.

I wasn't the only one being affected by the kiss, not if the hard bulge pressing against my nether regions was any indication.

Yep, Jack was more than a little aroused.

"Should we give you two privacy?" Rez asked, ever polite.

I didn't miss the nasty look Zon shot at Rez. "Why would you offer that? He seemed to enjoy watching me with Ari last night. Why should he get privacy if we want to watch our beautiful mate be pleasured?"

The whole having a harem thing was still weird to me, but heck! Just Zon talking about my mates watching each other take me was turning my insides into liquid lava.

Zon cocked his head and smirked at me. "Besides, our mate is excited by being watched."

Ducking my head, I tried to hide the deep ruby blush that was no doubt painting my cheeks… and probably my entire body.

Zon's chair scraped the floor as he scooted closer. His finger slid under my chin, lifting it so my eyes met his. "Look at me. Don't be embarrassed by anything you feel."

"Yes," Rez rumbled from across the table. "There is no shame in your desires. Take what you want from your mates. Let us please you, and let us enjoy watching your body be worshipped."

His words sent desire rushing through me like a tidal wave. I might've been able to hold in my moan... if Jack hadn't chosen that moment to run his hands across my stomach and up my ribs to cup my breasts. Even through my shirt, his touch had my body turning to jelly.

"Jack!" I moaned his name.

Encouraged by my reaction, Jack's hands disappeared under my skirt to tease along my outer thighs. Was he really going to take me right here? On a table I wasn't even sure could hold my weight?

Do you want him to wait until we return to the hotel and have a bed? Rez's words purred in my mind.

Hello kitty to the no! There wasn't a chance I wanted to wait to have him touching me... and filling me. Besides, it wasn't like this was the first table I'd been taken on.

I barely suppressed my shudder at the memory of how badly that had gone when my parents had walked in on that scene. They still weren't talking to me, but I didn't regret choosing my mates. Hopefully one day, they'd come around and be willing to talk with an open mind about my relationships.

But I wasn't going to hold my breath.

Shoving the depressing thoughts from my mind, I focused on Jack's hands as he explored my body.

"Rest your arms on the table and lean forward," Jack ordered, his voice low and demanding.

I obeyed, leaning forward until my forearms were flat

on the table and my backside was all but being presented to him.

Hooking his fingers under my thong's strap, he slid the silky fabric over my hips, letting it fall around my ankles. Wasting no time, Jack grabbed the hem of my skirt and flipped it up over my hips. He'd exposed me to his heated gaze.

I squirmed, partly from anticipation and partly from a belated sense of modesty. Reaching around, I tried to pull my skirt down to cover myself.

Twack.

"Ah!" I gasped, my butt cheek stinging. "Jack! Did you just spank me?"

"Yes, and I'll do it again if you try to hide yourself from me," Jack answered bluntly.

"But… But… you can't just do that!" I yelped.

The swat on my behind hadn't really hurt, but I couldn't believe he'd done it.

Jack leaned forward, his body pressing mine into the table. His chest rumbled. "Tell me to stop, and I'll stop."

His hand slid between my legs, stroking and teasing. I opened my mouth to tell him he couldn't just have his way with me, but his finger slipped inside me, and my train of thought took a sharp detour down Lust Lane.

"Do you want me to stop, Ari?" Jack nipped at my earlobe, his finger flicking against my clit.

"Ohhh. Please. N-no," I stammered, unable to form a complete sentence.

Jack trailed kisses down my neck as he slid a second

finger inside me. "What do you want?" I trembled beneath him, my body telling him everything he wanted to know, but still, Jack pushed for me to answer. "Tell me what you want, Arizona."

I rocked my hips against his hand, whimpering when he ground his palm against me, giving me the friction I desperately craved.

"Words. Use your words." Jack's teeth teased my skin.

"I… ugh. I—" My throat was tight, and I struggled to speak. "I need you inside me."

There was a snap as Jack removed his belt, followed by the rustle of fabric as he slid down his zipper.

What was taking him so long? Unable to help myself, I squirmed.

Jack's husky chuckle had me growing wetter.

His calloused palm slipped under my skirt and pressed low on my stomach as he held me still. Jack used his right hand to line his length up with my slick entrance.

I'd expected him to bury himself inside me with a single hard thrust, but he didn't. With infinite self-control, he slid in inch by excruciatingly slow inch into my silky heat.

My heart pounded in my ears as he drove me insane. Stretching me, filling me, completing me. Jack might not be the same size as my shifters, but there was no doubt his body was a perfect fit with mine.

Jack's steady, smooth rhythm stoked the flames of desire into an aching need. My body was still tender from being claimed by Zon, and my eyes pricked with tears.

He was fully in charge, but at the same time, Jack was reminding me how it felt to be made love to. It was as though time didn't exist, and there was nowhere else in the world we needed to be.

Lust knotted in my stomach, growing tauter with each of Jack's long, steady strokes. My nails scraped against the table as my breathing grew more ragged.

"Jack," I moaned, my body moving ever closer to the precipice.

"Come for me, Firefly," Jack whispered against my neck.

That was all it took for me to fall apart, losing myself in ecstasy as Jack continued to thrust inside me. I whimpered, unable to form words as I rode the waves of pleasure.

My walls tightened around Jack's hard erection, milking and squeezing until he finally lost control. Growling my name, his arms wrapped around my waist. Jack held me against him while our chests heaved and hearts thundered in unison.

When at last we caught our breath, Jack took his time buckling his pants before pulling off his shirt to clean me up. My heart swelled with love as I watched him. How did I get such caring mates?

When he finished, Jack sat down in his chair and pulled me onto his lap.

"What are you doing?" I laughed.

Jack smiled, his eyes shining with affection. "I'm cuddling you."

"You're injured."

I jumped at Rez's words. Somehow, I'd forgotten anyone else was in the room.

Rez rose from his seat and moved to squat in front of me. "You kicked at the table, and a piece of wood embedded itself in your leg."

"That's odd. I didn't feel a thing."

Zonkut's chuckle was dark. "Oh, you were feeling things, but pain wasn't one of them."

It was a reminder they'd watched the entire thing.

"I couldn't take my eyes off you," Rez answered my unspoken thoughts, lust heavy in his gaze as he looked up at me.

I was saved from answering when Albert pranced into view. He carried his semi-stolen souvenir in his mouth as he made his way to where I sat on Jack's lap.

Rez touched the splinter in my leg. "It's deep, so it will hurt when I pull it free. I'm sorry, my queen."

"Just get it out, Rez. It hurts more in my leg. I just hope I don't get tetanus from it." My growl turned to a hiss when my sexy dino-mate pinched the splinter and quickly yanked it from my skin.

Glancing down, I watched the thin trickle of crimson blood trail down my leg toward my ankle.

"Be still. I'll heal it." Rez moved his hand to cover the wound, but not before Albert shoved his nose against my thigh.

When Albert backed away, his newest treasure was smeared with my blood.

The weird scent of ozone flooded the room, and light flared.

"Shield them!" Rez roared.

He and Zon moved at a supernatural speed to tackle Jack and me away from the table just as an explosion shook the warehouse. Zon's arms wrapped around me, protecting me as the blast threw us into the unforgiving wall of the warehouse.

My scrambled brain was slow to comprehend the situation, but when realization finally dawned, it turned my blood to ice.

Albert had pulled off a ham heist at the museum.

It was as obvious as the horn on the Triceratops' nose in front of me that Albert's bone wasn't a replica at all.

It was the real mother-trucking deal, and the magic in my blood had just activated one of Tsufnu's spells.

CHAPTER ELEVEN
-ARIZONA-

What is a dinosaur's least favorite reindeer?
COMET!

"No, no, no!" I screamed, choking on the dust in the air. "This can't be happening! Not again!"

Albert Einswine might as well change his name to Chris P. Bacon... because that is what he was going to be after I got my hands on him.

"Shh. Calm down. It will be all right," Rez grunted, pushing away from the floor where he'd tackled Jack.

Zon's arms tightened around me. "Bro! Have you learned nothing? Those words produce the opposite effect in human females."

The chaos of the world faded away when I caught sight of the pieces of wood sticking out from Rez's arms and back. Dark blood was already seeping around the wounds, soaking through his pale blue T-shirt.

"Rez! You're injured!" I rolled out from beneath Zon's body and rushed to my injured mate's side.

An eardrum-shattering bellow shook the floor, sending me tumbling to my knees. I turned my head just in time to see the newly awakened dinosaur—that I'd somehow forgotten about—thundering toward me.

Covering my head, I braced for what was likely to be a fatal blow, but it never came.

With a battle call of unrestrained fury, Rez moved faster than my mind could process. Shifting into his Tyrannosaurus, he stepped over me, shielding me from the stampeding Triceratops.

His block would have worked if the newest dino hadn't shifted with blurring speed into their human form and slid beneath Rez's legs. For the second time in so many minutes, I found myself being tackled to the ground.

Hitting the concrete with enough force to knock the wind from my lungs, all I could think was, *why on earth does my grandmother's gift want to kill me?*

I'm not trying to kill you, jeertelk. I'm saving you from the men who were attacking you.

There was a feminine voice in my mind, and it didn't belong to me, myself, or I.

My eyes flew open, and I came face-to-face with a woman.

"You're female!" My brain was struggling to keep up with the curveballs life kept on throwing. What the heck was going on?

The woman grabbed my arm and pulled me into an

upright position. "Last I checked, I was." She spun around, crouching in front of me.

"Back away from Arizona," Zon commanded, his voice vibrating with fury.

His muscles tensed as he prepared to launch himself at the new shifter if she made any move to injure me.

"Dhoc zizan fesi. Mesrac akeel bhovu scaivlis." Venom dripped from her words.

"What is going on?" I screamed, growing more confused with each second that ticked by.

Apparently, I couldn't even understand English now. Maybe I had a concussion.

I told the shifter male to leave, and I'd let him live.

Great. The voice was back.

I was sent here to protect you.

"She said she is here to protect me!" I yelled to my mates.

My eardrums vibrated with the heavy bass of Rez's growl. *Who does she think she is to claim you need protection from us?* Rez's fury had his words banging around in my skull.

"We are her mates. Arizona doesn't need anyone else protecting her." Zon stalked toward us with his eyes glowing and his pupils thin slits. "If you do not back away, you'll need protection."

"Mates?" the female asked, stumbling over the pronunciation.

My brain, which had been knocked off-line, jumped back online. I'd just awakened a third dinosaur shifter, who'd nearly squashed me, before turning into a naked woman—

The woman was in her birthday suit.

"AHH! You're naked!" I screeched, covering my eyes.

Then I realized my mates were also seeing the woman, and my eyes snapped open.

There's nothing quite like jealousy to really clear the head of everything that's important. It latched onto the fact that there was a nude chick standing in front of my mates, and I was the only woman I wanted them to be looking at.

"Look away!" I screamed at my mates.

Jack's gaze was already firmly on the ground. Zon merely raised a questioning brow, and the massive T-Rex cocked his head to the side like a curious puppy.

"Why?" Zon asked. My reaction had temporarily distracted him from his rage.

"Because she's naked!" I pointed out the obvious. My eyes scanned the room, searching for something to cover her with.

I wasn't a prude, but it turned out I had a jealous streak wider than the entire state of Texas when it came to my mates.

Rez's amused laughter rumbled in my mind, and I tilted my head back to see that the T-Rex had closed his eyes. *I won't turn around, because I need to be able to snatch her from you if she attacks. But I will not look at her if that is what you wish, my queen.*

While Rez was taking my irrational reaction in stride, Zon was utterly baffled by it.

"Seriously? You're worried we'd desire another woman?" Zon didn't bother trying to hide his exasperation. "Ari, we are your mates! It's impossible for us to view another woman with desire."

You are the only woman our bodies will ever crave, Rez added through the link. *Only you.*

"Ari, nudity doesn't mean anything among shifters. I forgot how sensitive humans are about these things." Zon's eyes never left my face.

I was well aware I was overreacting, but my mates were the best thing to come into my life, and I was absolutely terrified of anything—or any*one*—who might take them away from me.

Never, Rez swore in my mind, turning the single word into a gentle caress.

Zonkut didn't speak. Instead, he moved forward. He didn't even acknowledge the hiss of the female shifter as he shoved past her to lift me into his arms.

Capturing my lips with his, Zon kissed me until my heart galloped, and I was light-headed. When he finally pulled away, my lips felt raw and puffy.

"Humans and shifters view the world differently. That is to be expected. But Ari, you need to realize you are our entire world. There will never be another mate for us. Only you." Zon's eyes were uncharacteristically soft as he pleaded with me not to question their devotion.

"Humans might be different from shifters, but in this case, I feel the same as the shifters." Jack had stood from the floor and moved to stand behind me until I was sandwiched between him and Zon. "There will never be another woman for me, either. You hold our hearts."

Oh! These men are your mates, not a threat to you. Ancients! I really got that one wrong, huh? the feminine voice drifted through my mind.

Fantastic. Now I'd get to listen to her ramblings as well as my own.

Can you hear her? I asked my mates through the bond.

Hear who? Rez asked. *The female?*

So, they couldn't hear her. Interesting.

"Set me down, please," I told Zon.

Giving both him and Jack a kiss, I pointed to the small break room at the back of the warehouse. "Rez needs to shift. You guys go wait back there for us."

"But what if she attacks you?" Zon asked, jerking his head in the woman's direction but carefully keeping his eyes locked with mine.

With a snort, she rattled off a series of clicks, trills, and harsh syllables.

My mouth fell open at the barrage. "What did she say?"

Zon, unfazed by her outburst, rolled his eyes. "She assured us, rather violently, that no harm would come to you. Apparently, she couldn't promise the same for us if we didn't start obeying you."

Laughing, I gave Jack and Zon a gentle shove toward the door. "I'll be fine. Go on."

Reluctantly, my men turned their backs on us and moved away.

As soon as I was sure the guys were in the break room, I

hurried to the corner where I'd left a single suitcase. Most of our stuff was at the hotel, but I'd left a few spare items at the warehouse in case of an emergency... or in case the guys got naughty and ripped my clothing accidentally—or not so accidentally.

Rifling through my garments, I found a T-shirt and a loose pair of gym shorts. She was several inches shorter than me, but while I had willowy form, this chick definitely ate all her Wheaties. I wouldn't be surprised to find out she was a bodyguard or a bouncer.

I figured the stretchy shorts and oversized shirt would fit her okay, at least until we were able to figure out what we were going to do with her. I wanted to smack myself when I realized I'd made her sound like a stray puppy or a lost kitten that needed to find a home.

Stifling a laugh, I tried really hard to think about anything other than what the found dinosaur posters might look like.

Once she'd dressed, I led her to the break area. The room was empty other than some cheap plastic lawn chairs and a table with a TV so ancient it might be older than my shifter mates.

Zon shot me a narrow-eyed glare, giving away that he'd been listening to my thoughts. I really should practice blocking them out more. While I could do it, long-term maintenance of the shield caused terrible migraines.

Please don't block us out all the time, my queen, Rez sent the thought. *We like hearing your thoughts and knowing you are safe and happy.*

Blowing him a kiss, I didn't allow myself to be side-tracked.

I guided our new friend into a chair before settling myself in the chair nearest her, ready to jump between my mates and the woman if things went south.

Scanning the room, I searched for the problematic pork, but he'd wisely chosen to stay out of my line of sight. He was wise for one so small.

"Okay, let's sort this mess out." Focusing my attention on the blonde-haired female, I asked the most important question. "What's your name?"

There was a pause, and you could almost see the wheels turning behind her pale green eyes as she processed my words.

Finally, she spoke. "My name is Sulseti."

"Sull-se-tee," I said out loud, wincing when it came out more stilted than Sulseti's speech. "That's really pretty."

Sulseti gave me a smile. "Call me Suli."

I couldn't help but laugh. She'd found a polite way to tell me I had butchered the pronunciation. "That is probably for the best until I practice it more in private. I'm Arizona, but you can call me Ari."

Yes, I am aware, she giggled, reverting to speaking in the mental link.

While her spoken words were stiff, she was adjusting to modern language faster than Rez or Zon. Was she sorting through my thoughts to learn? Just like the men had done when they first awakened?

Yes. It is the quickest way. Her soft voice once again drifted through my mind.

Fragglerock-crackle-pop! I was never going to have privacy in my brain again at this rate.

Blowing out a sigh, I pointed to each man in turn. "And this is Jack, Rezkac, and Zonkut. My mates."

Suli tilted her head, studying each man in turn, her eyes glowing. "Three mates?"

"Yes." My cheeks warmed from a combination of pride and shyness. Other than my parents—who only knew about Rez and Zon—this was the first time I'd claimed the men as mine to someone else.

"One is human?" she questioned, her brow furrowing.

"Yes. I'm human," Jack answered.

Suli's eyes studied my shifter mates. "You accept this?"

Rez shrugged. "Of course. If it makes Arizona happy, then we have no issue with it."

"Although I could live without the tiny demon," Zon mumbled under his breath, low enough that Suli didn't seem to catch it.

"Suli?" I asked, drawing her attention back to me. "Why are you here?"

I really hoped she wasn't about to tell me she was my mate. Sulseti seemed nice, but I certainly didn't feel the pull of a mate bond with her.

"To be your B-F-F." Suli emphasized each letter, giving me the distinct impression she had been coached on exactly how to answer my question.

I pursed my lips. "Do you know what a BFF is?"

Her expression lit up, and a brilliant smile spread across her face as she responded in my mind. *Yes! I was bound to be your friend for your full lifespan.*

Alrighty then.

That wasn't creepy… not at all.

"Bound to me by my grandmother?" I pressed, trying to figure out what my granny had been thinking.

I need to respond telepathically. It's easier to answer in your mind while my tongue becomes accustomed to your language. Tsufnu wanted me to be your friend. Suli's expression turned sad. She explained that our world was filled with connections. *Humans, in your time, are able to speak with anyone they want, no matter what part of the world they are in. Yet humans are lonely.*

I opened my mouth to tell her I wasn't lonely and explained that humans nowadays have tons of friends, but then I closed it. Tsufnu was right. As a species, we had lost the art of making friends, and of how to be a good friend.

How long had it been since I'd had a best friend? Fourth grade? Maybe eighth grade? I'd been terribly lonely until Albert and my mates came into my life.

Tsufnu also said you can't live in a house full of men without a female bestie to confide in, Suli added, giving me a sly grin. *That is why she used her magic to create this special link in our minds. It blocks your mates from hearing us. You can complain about them, and they will never know. Won't that be fun?*

"Is she talking to Arizona through a mind link?" Jack asked Rez and Zon, leaning toward me slightly. "That's the same face Arizona makes when she talks with you two."

"That would be highly unusual—" Rez began, only to be cut off by Zon.

"I think Jack's right. They are talking in a mental link." Zon squinted, looking between Suli and me with suspicion. "I can't hear anything in Arizona's mind. How is this possible?"

"Suli says my grandmother's magic created a mental link between us." I shrugged. Magic and how it worked was well above my pay grade at that point, so I had no idea how Tsufnu had done this.

Rez nodded. "She was powerful, more than capable of creating such a link."

"But why?" Zon asked, his eyes sparking with wariness.

Suli's lips twitched. "Because boys suck."

CHAPTER TWELVE
-ARIZONA-

Why did the brontosaurus devour the factory?
BECAUSE SHE WAS A PLANT-EATER

I couldn't help it. I burst out laughing. And I continued laughing until tears were streaming down my face.

"Why would you say that?" I wheezed, still trying to get my giggles under control.

The fact my men wore matching stony-faced expressions only added to my amusement.

Suli shot me a mischievous smile. *Tsufnu told me to say that when your mates questioned my purpose.*

"You're here to convince our mate she doesn't need us?" Zon asked, his words a rumbling thunder that promised a coming storm.

Suli screwed up her face. "No. I am her friend."

Zon's tense muscles relaxed.

"And to protect her if you fail," Suli added, aggravating him all over again.

"We can protect our mate. We don't need your help," Zon snarled, shoving out of his chair.

Rez grabbed his shirt, hauling him backward. "Calm down, Zonkut. Priestess Tsufnu didn't make mistakes. We share the goal of making sure Arizona is happy and keeping her safe. There is no reason for us to be angry."

He's an emotional mess, yes? Suli asked through our private link. *Typical raptor.*

"All right. Everyone settle down." Jack used his reassuring detective tone. "Let's talk this through… calmly."

Rez and I nodded. Huffing, Zon flopped back down in his plastic chair.

"Suli, you're a dinosaur shifter, too, correct?" Jack, ever a detective at heart, started with the easy questions. He probably hoped to ease into the harder stuff without her noticing.

"Yes."

"She's what humans now call a Triceratops," Rez supplied helpfully.

"That's amazing!" Jack smiled at Suli. "And you are one of Arizona's gifts from her grandmother? Tsufnu wanted you to be a friend and bodyguard for Ari?"

"Correct." Suli nodded, picking at the fabric of the cotton shorts.

"Why would you agree to be bound to me? What about a family, or a fated mate you wanted to stay with? I can't imagine being willing to give up my whole life for a stranger."

Suli smiled at me. *I had no family that wished to claim me. Sons are the pride of my family. I was born a daughter, and was never able to atone for that shortcoming. I became a wanderer, and traveled to many places. Then I met the Priestess. She claimed me as her granddaughter and refused to let me leave. She showered me with the love I'd always wanted from a family. When she talked about you, I saw heard the pride and the concern she felt. I knew when she passed away, I would be alone again. So, I asked to be bond to you in a bond of friendship and protection.*

I repeated what she's told me to the others. Then turned back to her, "So I'm just a way to repay the kindness she showed you?"

Suli burst into laughter. *No. She let me travel with her in visions sometimes, and I felt like I got to know you, like you were my friend too. And I saw Tsufnu in you. After I asked, Tsufnu told me that I will find my fated mate on the path I'd chosen. This is where I am meant to be.*

"I'm glad you're here." I grinned. "And I wonder where your fated mate is."

Suli shrugged; *we will find him when the time is right.*

"We can't hear what is said in the link between you two. Can Sulseti hear what we say in our link?" Zon asked, still sulking.

I didn't know the answer to that and raised a brow in Suli's direction.

"No." Suli hesitated, trying to find the words. "Tsufnu

used her magic to make sure it is a private link between Ari's mind and mine."

Her words were becoming less stilted with each word she spoke. It was incredible how quickly the shifters were able to adjust to modern language.

A new thought drifted into my mind, chilling my blood as horror flooded through me. If Suli was sifting through my thoughts like Rez and Zon were able to, was she seeing my thoughts related to the sexy times I shared with my mates?

Suli burst out laughing. *No, I see no specifics about breeding with your mates. I do not understand why humans are shy when it comes to mating. Why do you all pretend you do not mate? Sex is a need. It is the same as if humans all pretended they did not consume food. But the priestess said it was necessary to ensure you had complete privacy with your mind during those times.*

Relieved, I blew out the air I'd been holding in my lungs. I didn't care if she thought it was weird. My time with my guys wasn't something I wanted her accidentally finding in my memories.

"So basically, I have a new bestie." I looked at my shifter mates. "I can barely keep you two hidden! How am I supposed to keep another dinosaur safe?"

My pulse began to race as anxiety strolled into my mind, ready to push me over the edge into full-blown panic.

"We are here to keep you safe," Suli spoke each word carefully. "Why would you need to protect us?"

I bit my lip, trying to decide how to explain the challenges I'd faced when it came to keeping a handle on my dinosaurs delicately. "Um…"

Rez saved me by answering her question bluntly. "You'll find that the stimuli and chaos of this world, the Vazi's magic Arizona possesses, and our beasts' natural instincts… together, those things make it very difficult to keep control of your form."

Suli's face crumpled in confusion. She didn't understand what Rez was trying to say.

"We keep losing our crap, okay?" Zon answered bluntly.

"You're not going to feel the mate pull, which might help you stay more stable. But if you were assigned as a guardian, you're going to have trouble maintaining control every single time you feel she is under possible attack, or at risk of being hurt."

"So, this world makes our beasts hard to handle?" Suli questioned.

Rez and Zon nodded.

"Last night, we lost control because a gentleman touched Arizona, and we felt he was disrespecting her. Things were a little bit of a mess after that." Rez scrubbed a hand down his face.

Jack burst out laughing. "A little? That's like saying hell might be a little warm. You two reenacted a scene straight out of a dinosaur apocalypse film," Jack croaked out between laughs. "It was insanity. Pure, unadulterated insanity. And it's a wonder we're not all in jail right now for disrupting the peace, risking life and limb, or for damaging private property."

"If Theresa realizes the little ham heisted a real dinosaur bone from the museum, we may still face legal trouble," I grumbled, scanning the room for a familiar peach-skinned piglet.

I tried to look annoyed, but Jack's laughter was contagious, and the corner of my mouth began to twitch.

We'd figure things out. I mean, it's not like things could get any worse.

The moment I thought those words, I tried to un-think them, but it was too late.

It was as though I'd spoken the magic words of an ancient curse. Because every time I said them, I unleashed the power of Pandora's box in my life.

Albert Einswine darted into the room with a squeal, weaving between the legs of the chairs as he did laps around the room.

Rez stiffened, doing his best impression of a stone statue, hoping Albert wouldn't notice him. Zon tried to scramble away but failed spectacularly. His chair flipped over, dumping him onto the floor.

Delighted by how successfully he was terrorizing the dinos, Albert darted beneath Sulseti's chair. I would have preferred to find a different way to introduce Suli to Albert, but that ship had just sailed away.

"Demon!" she shrieked. "Get away from her."

One minute, the muscular blonde was sitting in the chair next to me, and the next, she'd shifted into her gray

Triceratops form. She snorted, stomping the concrete while trying to block Albert from reaching me.

"Suli, it's okay!" I cried, trying to rush past her to grab Albert.

Instead of trying to save his bacon like a smart little pig, Albert squared up with the dinosaur equivalent of a giant rhinoceros.

Snorting in challenge, Albert Einswine pawed the ground like a tiny bull ready to charge.

What had I eaten or drunk today that could have me hallucinating? Because surely, that was the only logical explanation for the absurd scene playing out in front of me.

With a Spartan warrior-worthy squeal, Albert charged.

Was he really delusional enough to believe he was the same size as the dinos? If it had been Zon or Rez, they would've tucked tail and run. But Suli wasn't one to run from any type of fight. I doubted it boded well for our future.

Rushing around her, I managed to snatch Albert, saving him from himself. The riled-up Triceratops roared with rage behind me.

It's okay, Suli! I shouted in my mind, hoping I found the right link. *He's a pet. He belongs to me.*

The Triceratops wasn't going to be placated or reassured. With another furious bellow, she charged after us.

Deciding the best course of action when it came to Albert was out of sight, out of mind, I rushed for the front door of the warehouse. If I could take Albert outside, it would give Suli time to calm down. Then I could explain things to her.

And this was where the 'things can't get worse' part of my curse decided to kick things up a notch. Because as I flung open the front door, I came face-to-face with Teresa.

#

Teresa's expression changed from surprise to delight, then back to surprise again.

She was shocked?

Well, that made two of us.

"Uh. Hi?" I squeaked, yanking the door closed behind me and barreling into her.

"Is that a Triceratops?" Teresa asked, trying to peer around me as I slammed the door closed.

An instant later, there was an eardrum-bursting crash as Suli's massive body slammed into the warehouse wall. The metal groaned and shrieked as it bent to form an outline of my brand-spanking-new dino bestie.

"Yes. It is. My programmer and I are working out some kinks. But Albert needed to go on a little walk to relieve himself. You know how it is with tiny bladders," I rambled, ignoring the grunt of annoyance from the pig I clutched in my arms.

Teresa's eyes dropped to Albert, then flicked back to the dinosaur-shaped outline in the warehouse wall. "I didn't realize you had a third dinosaur."

Shifting Albert under one arm, I used my right hand to guide Teresa away from the warehouse. The last thing I needed was for her to suggest we go inside.

"As you can see, we are still working out some… bugs," I finished lamely.

Teresa continued to cast glances over her shoulder.

"I'm assuming you didn't stop by just to say hi?" I prompted, hoping to bring her back to the reason behind the visit and distract her from the ongoing catastrophe that was my life.

Teresa shook her head to clear it and met my eyes. "You left this in my office, and I thought I'd drop it by."

She held out a familiar-looking wallet.

Since I'd walked to and from the museum, I hadn't needed it to book a ride. But how had I completely forgotten it? Oh yeah. Because Albert had decided we should run an impromptu 5k marathon inside the museum.

"Thank you so much for bringing it to me. If you'd called me, I could have come back to the museum and saved you the trouble, though!"

Teresa waved away my thanks. "It was no problem. Truly."

Sitting Albert on the grass, I patted his butt. "Go potty."

Albert sat on his hindquarters and gave me a condescending glare. If he'd been human, he would have thrown me the bird.

"There was one more thing." Teresa looked embarrassed. "I know I said I would give you time to discuss Bartholomew's offer with your bosses, but I wanted to tell you privately how much this would mean to the museum."

Ignoring Albert's disgruntled expression, I smiled up at

Teresa. "I do understand. It would be great for the museum and the local community."

Teresa's face lit up with excitement. "Yes, and it could open the door to other sponsorships and summer programs. I've found that if one local business makes a large donation for an exhibit, others quickly follow."

When I didn't immediately respond, Teresa's smile faltered. "Please tell me you are still considering it, and you aren't about to tell me the answer is no?"

Leaning down, I scratched behind Albert's ear. "Dino-vation hasn't said no, but they do have some restrictions they'd like you and Bartholomew to review. I'll email them over before the end of the day."

Teresa clapped her hands together, then caught herself and clasped them at her waist. "I understand. Okay, I'll leave you alone to enjoy your day, and I'll watch for your email."

CHAPTER THIRTEEN
-ARIZONA-

What dinosaur loves pancakes?
A TRI-SYRUP-TOPS.

We woke the next morning to an email from Teresa letting me know that each of our requirements and revisions to the proposal had been accepted.

Apparently, Teresa had spilled the beans about our newest 'prototype' to Bartholomew and the museum board, because the email included a jaw-dropping five-figure bonus if we'd include the third robotic dinosaur in the program.

How could we refuse an offer like that? Besides, it solved a dilemma we'd been worried about. It wasn't as though we could leave Suli in a dino daycare while we worked the summer camp program.

However, there was no way I could leave her in the

warehouse alone. Who knows what trouble she might find? And there was always the possibility Bartholomew's minions might be lurking around.

I was apprehensive about taking a newly awakened shifter in public, but at least we had two weeks to get Suli up to speed on the world outside the warehouse. We could give her a crash course on modern etiquette before the exhibit started. I just hoped she was a quick learner.

Clicking open the attached documents, I found Teresa had made things easy by attaching two copies of the contract. One had only two dinos included in the agreement, and the other mentioned three.

With a trembling hand, I added the necessary signatures as Dinovation's official representative. Feeling fairly confident that despite our precautions, this was going to backfire spectacularly, I attached the signed agreement and hit send on the email.

Not even fifteen minutes later, the museum deposited an advance into our bank account that was equal to my previous yearly salary. Shoving away from the desk, I spun around to face the three shifters and one human who watched me with keen interest.

"Well, it's a done deal! We better start getting Sulseti used to being in public."

While I had reservations about our decision, it was also nice to not feel worried about our family's immediate financial future. We didn't have to mooch off Jack, and could breathe a little easier.

And who knew?

It might even be fun.

#

With only two weeks before the summer camp program, we had worked from morning until evening trying to desensitize Suli to the overwhelming sights and sounds she'd encounter in the modern world... all while trying to adjust to our new five-person dynamic.

We couldn't have her losing it amid a group full of kids. I shivered in horror, imagining her giant triceratops body plowing through them like a bowling ball, while tiny humans flew through the air like bowling pins.

Zon snickered, and I scowled at him.

"What? I don't want children injured, but your mental images are vivid and highly amusing. Far better than TV." He gave me a saucy smile.

"There are only two days left before we need to report to the museum for a trial run-through. So today we are taking Suli to the park one last time to make sure she's made enough progress to be comfortable around people for eight hours a day."

Suli's face lit with excitement, but Zon and Rez exchanged wary glances.

Jack scratched behind Albert's ear and grinned. "This is bound to be entertaining."

That was reassuring.

Not.

"Suli, you are doing amazing, but it is hard to forget that on one of those outings, you tried to eat trash. And then growled at the dog walkers we passed." Rez was being kind.

Saying it hadn't gone well was putting it mildly. It had been an absolute flustercuck.

We'd only been outside the warehouse for an hour, when Suli caught a whiff of a hamburger and leaped into a dumpster. She'd already devoured half of the burger before we'd managed to pry her, kicking and hissing, from the garbage.

Dragging her back to the warehouse had been horrible because she reeked of trash, which is what had drawn the attention of every dog we passed.

Still irritated at having her snack taken, Suli had growled at the dogs, who were staring at her while licking their chops. When the owners noticed her threatening their pets, it hadn't gone well. A few decided to throw insults her way, and I guess I shouldn't have been surprised when she lunged for them, ready to throw hands.

"At least it can't be—" I quickly stopped myself from finishing that particular sentence. "Besides, she's not had an incident since last week."

"Except for the ice cream cone she snatched from that bratty kid in the stroller three days ago," Jack added helpfully.

"How was I supposed to know modern communities are not good at sharing?" Suli spoke the words carefully, her tongue still getting used to the English language. "Now I understand that it is frowned upon to take food without asking. It's strange that humans don't like sharing, but find it acceptable to throw good food in the trash. Such an odd species."

What was I supposed to say to that?

She was right, after all. Humans were horribly wasteful.

I clapped my hands and wrangled my protesting mates toward the door. "Okay. Let's head to the park. It shouldn't be too crowded right now. The kids will get out of school in about three hours, and the park will get pretty busy. That will be a good final test to make sure she is ready to tolerate the summer camp kids."

I wished I could've given Suli more time to get used to the modern world before throwing her in head-first, but it was time for her to sink or swim.

We'd run out of time.

#

There were only a few people at the park, so we took our time walking the two-mile loop that circled a large pond and the playgrounds.

I glanced toward the basketball court to check on my mates and grinned at what I saw. While Zon and Rez might not understand how to play card games, they'd taken to basketball like dung beetles to a turd.

Jack was in perfect athletic shape, but he couldn't keep up with the powerful dinos. He had stopped to rest, and watched Rez and Zon toss the ball with careless ease toward the hoop... from the opposite side of the court. And nearly every toss would swish through the net.

"Why don't you just go breed them? You will both feel

better, and then you can stop drooling on your face while you watch them." Suli rolled her eyes.

"I've already told you, breeding—I mean, sex—isn't like it was the last time you walked the Earth. We'd end up arrested if we did some of the stuff it sounds like you got away with." The mental image of walking over to Jack and jumping on for a ride had me blushing furiously.

Suli's eyebrows drew together. "It's just so weird to me that you're embarrassed by the thought of breeding with your mates. I'd understand better if they were strangers to you, but they aren't. Jack is human, so he might not be willing. But I am positive if you walked over to either of your shifters right now, you could mount them, and they would not complain and would see that your needs were met."

The memory of Rez and Zon fingering me under the table in the restaurants flashed through my mind. They'd had no problems taking care of my needs, and they'd continued talking and eating while bringing me to my climax. They were respectful of my need for privacy, though.

"Are human males as shy as females about sex?" Suli asked. Before I could answer, her eyes widened, and a smile stretched across her heavily freckled face. "I know! There is a guy standing by the water. I'll present myself and see—"

I looped my arm through hers. "Oh, no you're not! That will get you locked up."

Probably. For all I knew, that guy might be into it.

"Locked up for meeting a need we both have? This is so unusual." Suli was struggling to wrap her mind around the concept. "Maybe that is why so many humans are frowning and unhappy. They are deprived of the ability to care for their most basic needs."

How had she managed to make it sound like humans were the strange ones for wanting to keep sex—mostly—in the privacy of one's home? She made it sound like it was no different from grabbing a snack or fast food. If you desired it, and the other party was willing, it was acceptable.

"There is an exception. We don't breed others once we are claimed by our mate. After being claimed, our body just doesn't desire any others. Unless a person has more than one mate, like you." Suli stopped to inspect a butterfly bush's blooms, before continuing to walk.

I'm not sure where the conversation might have gone if the robotic tin can music of an ice-cream truck growing louder hadn't distracted us. Deciding I could use a cool down, I had Suli sit on a bench, and I went to meet the truck and secure treats for the five of us.

Several kids beat me to the truck, and I waited in line for almost ten minutes before finally being handed five ice cream cones in a cardboard carrying tray. I eagerly made my way back to the bench where I'd left Suli, only to find her gone. Maybe she went to join the guys?

Trying not to knock the cones from the holder, I jogged toward the ball court... but she wasn't there either.

"Have you seen Suli? I left her on a bench but couldn't find her." I handed the cones to the guys while my eyes scanned the park.

When I recognized her thick blonde braid talking to a

guy as they walked toward the parking lot, my heart dropped to my toes.

"Suli!" I screamed her name and darted down the path toward her. I should have reached out through the mental link, but that didn't occur to me until later. All I could think about then was getting to her as quickly as possible.

Catching up to the laughing pair, I wondered if the talk about sex had affected her to the point she decided to take care of what she considered a basic need.

"Suli!" I wheezed, holding my side and trying not to wince at the cramp in my side.

She looked over her shoulder, and her eyes widened. "Are you okay? Why are you running?"

"Where are you going? I thought you were going to wait on the bench." I leaned against a car, trying to quiet my breathing to hide the fact that I was out of shape and fighting for my life.

I wasn't actually dying, but I don't think my body knew that.

"I was waiting, and then Lars sat down next to me. We talked, and look, Arizona! He gave me these!" She opened her hand to show me various brightly colored candies.

My eyes shot to Lars's face, and the way his eyes darted around gave me the distinct impression he was nervous and afraid to be caught doing what he was doing.

Guys? Don't panic, but I might need backup, I sent through the link.

When I said nothing out loud, but continued staring Lars down, Suli continued, "It's candy! And it tastes amazing! Lars said he has more in his van and offered to get me some if I'd walk with him. Isn't that nice?"

"Suli, I want you to step away from Lars and come with me. NOW," I ordered.

She stubbornly set her jaw. "I'll meet you down by the court, just let me get—"

"Suli! This is Stranger Danger 101! You don't ever get anywhere near the van! Just like you don't follow red balloons anywhere near sewer drains. He's probably going to kidnap you."

I left the girl for ten minutes and she was already climbing into a rusted-out white van that couldn't be any more suspicious unless he wrote 'free candy inside' on the sides.

"Lars wouldn't do that! Would you—" Suli turned to face him, only to see him sprinting away.

He knew the jig was up.

The guys ran up beside us. "Want me to chase him down?" Rez asked, not the least bit out of breath.

"No need." Jack lifted his phone, snapped a picture, and texted it to someone. "I have some friends in the local precincts. They'll handle him."

Suli's expression was a heartbreaking mix of disappointment, confusion, and disbelief.

"Are you okay?"

She heaved a sigh, then answered. "I'm fine. It is disorienting to be awakened after so long. The rules are different. And the social cues are unfamiliar. It's a lot to learn and adjust to. I was bound to have a few lapses in judgment."

"I know." I wrapped my arm around her waist, happy I'd gotten to her in time.

At that thought, the shifters burst into loud guffaws.

"What are you three laughing at?" I demanded.

No one could answer at first, but finally, Suli managed to choke out, "You've forgotten I'm a shifter. He was more likely to be injured by me if he tried something!"

My indignation quickly faded into laughter. We all had a lot to learn and get used to.

CHAPTER FOURTEEN
-ARIZONA-

What kind of dinosaur can you ride in a rodeo?
A BRONCO-SAURUS!

The first three days of exhibits went off without a hitch, and so far, today had gone smoothly as well. But instead of feeling relieved, it was making me nervous. The other shoe was bound to drop any minute.

Bartholomew had stopped by on the second day to talk with Teresa, but he hadn't approached me or my dinos.

The only other hiccup had been a gardener who kept finding excuses to work as close as possible to the dinos' enclosures, but I hadn't figured out if he was trying to gather intel, or if he was just a huge dinosaur fan. Whatever the case, he hadn't crossed the fence into any of the exhibits while a dino was inside it.

"It's day four!" I wrapped my arms around Jack's waist. "Only three more days left in our contract after today!"

"It's actually been enjoyable." Jack kissed the top of my head. "Did you see the group of scouts this morning? I think half that troop will end up becoming paleontologists."

"I sure did. They asked harder questions than the college group from yesterday!" I laughed and pulled away to move closer to the fence around Zonkut's enclosure. "If Rez and Zon hadn't been giving me the answers telepathically, I'd have been in trouble."

The raptor stood and ambled toward me. When he was close enough, I leaned over the rail and scratched his forehead.

"It looks like someone is forgetting these are robotics and not pets."

I didn't need to turn around to recognize Bartholomew's grating voice. Well, there it was. The shoe had dropped.

"There is nothing wrong with appreciating a work of art." I patted Zon's nose and spun around to face my least favorite person on Earth.

Zonkut gave a low growl from behind me.

Bartholomew held out his hand, but Jack intercepted it and gave it a hearty shake. "Hi, I'm Jack, Arizona's fiancé. I don't think we've had the opportunity to meet."

I ducked my head to hide my smile. Jack knew the shifters didn't like Bartholomew near me, let alone touching me, and he'd skillfully kept them from stressing out.

"Uh, yes. Hello. Good to meet you." Bartholomew eyed me, but Jack stepped to the side, partially blocking his view.

"You've done a great thing sponsoring this program for the kids. There has been a steady stream of visitors every day, and the camp kids have such bright minds." Jack expertly managed to get Bartholomew to walk with him through the exhibit.

"Whew!" I sagged against the fence, only to jump away when the raptor—a.k.a. Zon—nipped my butt. "Hey! Not cool."

Several visitors wandering around nearby giggled at the exchange.

You see what you did? I snapped through the link.

The raptor widened his eyes, trying to appear innocent. *I'm just putting on a good show. That's what we're being paid for, right?*

BARTHOLOMEW SPENT the next two hours trying to approach me, only to be thwarted by Jack each and every time.

I can see why you picked the human male. He is able to handle people in a way we can't. Although I agree with Rezkac, it would be easier to just eat the man you dislike so strongly. Suli was way too casual about the concept of murder.

Eating people just because we don't like them isn't acceptable, I thought in the link.

Wow. Those were words I never thought I'd utter.

Eating people was wrong. End of story. And it was gross.

Suli giggled. *That's not what you think about being eaten by your mates.*

Horrified, I spun around to gape at the female triceratops. When she licked her lips, I choked on a strangled cry. If Suli had possessed brows in this form, I knew she would've been wiggling them suggestively.

"That's not… it's not the same!" I spluttered.

"What's not the same?" Bartholomew came to stand beside me, leaning against the fence.

I swallowed my groan. Suli had me so flustered I'd forgotten to reply through the link.

"And who are you talking to?" He scanned the surrounding area before giving me a strange look when he realized I was alone.

"I'm practicing lines for a theater performance." What the heck? Where had that come from?

"I didn't realize you were a performer, although I should have guessed after that dinner show you orchestrated." Bartholomew leaned against the fence so that he faced me. "What is the name of the performance?"

Thank goodness I'd been blessed with quick wits!

Oh, wait. I hadn't.

When they'd been handing out wit, I'd thought they said tits and asked for something subtle.

"Jurasissy Parock." Why the lines from the social media reel popped into my mind at that very moment, I'd never know.

When Bartholomew thankfully didn't get the joke, and continued to look confused at the vague reference, my trainwreck of a brain made the executive decision to double down on my lie.

Because of course it did.

"Rawr?"

Zon and Rez, who'd enjoyed rewatching a certain dinosaur movie franchise over and over, cackled like hens in the link.

From the corner of my eye, I caught sight of the raptor collapsing to the ground in laughter. Although, to a bystander, it probably looked more like he was having a coughing fit.

Meanwhile, the T-Rex was bobbing his head in amusement, in the same way a parrot might when excited by something. Rez's raucous barking laughter echoed around the park.

Is that truly your best roar? Suli's mouth dropped open, and the grass she'd been eating fell from her lips. *Tsufnu was right. You need me. At least you are young, so it is possible you can learn.*

Ignoring the obnoxious dino trio, I refocused my attention on Bart. It took everything in me to keep a straight face, but I managed. *Barely.*

"That sounds"—Bartholomew searched for the right word—"interesting."

"Oh, it most certainly is." I nodded, looking serious. "A work of literary genius."

I discreetly cast a look around, searching for Jack,

hoping he would haul Bartholomew away again. Where had he gone?

Bathroom, Zon provided, still chuckling.

Okay, I just had to survive a few minutes in Bart's company, then Jack would be back. I could do this.

"I've been trying to talk with you all morning, but you are quite the popular lady among the museum's guests." His smile was charming and meant to lower my defenses.

Instead, I went on red alert.

A charming snake was still a snake. And I trusted snakes a lot more than I trusted this greedy businessman.

Bart continued. "Scott has done some more research on Dinovation. It's quite an unusual company. He was unable to find out who is on the board, who is in charge of marketing, who does the programming, etc."

I schooled my features into a blank mask, letting him talk but giving nothing away.

He didn't seem to notice my silence. "Did you know that most companies want people to actually find out about them and their product? There's no way to turn a profit if potential clients have no way of contacting you."

Bart's eyes sharpened, a predator trying to find his prey's weakness.

Yeah, well, I slept soundly in the arms of the king of predators every night, so this pathetic attempt at intimidation was almost amusing.

"Which raises an interesting question. How can your company afford to do the necessary research, and purchase the necessary materials, to create advanced robotic prototypes?"

"Private funding," I answered automatically, having rehearsed the answer before we came to Texas.

"But even private investors would want reports of how their money is being used. And now that prototypes have been created, they're going to want a way to benefit from their original investments," Bartholomew pressed.

Dang. The man was like a dog with a bone.

A hard bone... for my dinosaurs.

He wants to have sex with dinosaurs? Suli gasped in the link. *Gross.*

No, he has a bone, not a boner, I corrected her.

I fail to see the difference, Suli snorted, taking a step away from Bart.

I tried again. *It's a euphemism—a saying. It means he is obsessed with getting his hands on my dinosaurs.*

Still creepy, Suli quipped.

She wasn't wrong. The man made my skin crawl. How was Teresa able to stomach being around him?

Bart hadn't noticed my distraction and had continued speaking. "Surely your backers are getting antsy for a return on their investments? I know I would be."

I gave him a tight smile. "Then I guess it's good you aren't an investor. We're thankful that our board sees our visions, which have nothing to do with profits. We are more interested in education."

Where was Jack?! How far was the bathroom?

Maybe he ate ice cream again? That doesn't settle well on his stomach… Suli suggested.

Don't mention that in front of Jack, he's sensitive about it, I warned her.

He's definitely sensitive about it. None of us could use the restroom for over an hour after he ate some last week. The triceratops shuddered.

"Scott also found something else interesting. Dinovation hasn't filed any patents on their prototypes or their techniques."

I raised an eyebrow as though to say, 'and?'

"Everyone in the industry knows patents are filed long before the public gets even a peek at the work a company is doing."

I'd had enough of the conversation and decided to save time by cutting to the chase. "Why are you so focused on how Dinovation does business? They agreed to your proposal for this event. You got what you wanted. Is there something else weighing on your mind?"

You go, girl! Suli cheered encouragement.

Rez stomped at the ground, and Zon paced the fence. They were growing agitated by the arrogant blowhard.

A slow smile spread across Bart's face. "It would be a shame if someone else filed those patents before Dinovation."

"I'll be sure to pass that suggestion on to the board," I ground out between gritted teeth. "If there is nothing else—"

"Actually, there is," he cut me off. "Come to dinner with

me tonight. There are only three days left of the event, and I'd like to discuss a business matter with you. Just the two of us."

Was he for real right now?

I darted a quick look around for Jack and spotted him talking with Teresa near the museum's door.

"I have dinner plans with my *fiancé* and team."

Bart cast a pointed glance at my bare finger. "Fiancé? Until there is a ring, your man has left room for another man to swoop in and woo his girl. I'm sure I could show you a night to remember in Texas."

The only activity I'd consider with this man was one involving me sticking my boot up his butt...

As soon as the thought flitted through my mind, Suli was charging at the fence. Bart had his back to her, so he didn't realize the triceratops was behind him.

The fence was made up of wrought iron bars, much like the old Victorian-era gates. So Suli was able to shove her horn between the bars, take aim, and stick her horn up his fudge-factory.

Bartholomew screeched, falling forward on his knees.

I clapped my hand over my mouth, preventing any sound from escaping. I truly didn't know if I'd start apologizing or laughing like a banshee, and I decided it was best not to risk it.

SULI! Tell me you did not just spear him in the anus?!

The unrepentant shifter rolled her eyes in a very un-dino-like manner. *No. That would be gross. I just poked him a bit and ripped through his pants.*

WHY WOULD YOU DO THAT? I rummaged through my pockets to find the fake remote and pretended to click buttons. *You better start pretending you're in sleep mode.*

This was your idea. And a good one, too. You wanted to stick your shoe up his backside; I was helping. Suli dropped to the ground, eyes still sparkling with amusement. *We're going to get along great, bestie.*

Evening out her breathing, Suli closed her eyes, and pretended to sleep.

"What is wrong with that robot? It could have killed me!" Bart roared, shoving himself off the concrete and twisting to inspect the damage to the seat of his pants.

Jack and Teresa hurried across the hot pavement to join us.

"Like we said, this is our newest prototype, and she's still got a few kinks."

You bet I do, Suli snickered.

I was beginning to think she was having selective English misunderstandings, just so she could do whatever she wanted—and then act innocent after the fact.

"Come with me. We keep some extra clean garments in our office closet." Teresa took Bart's arm and began leading him toward the museum.

He glanced over his shoulder. "Arizona, think about it."

I forced a smile on my face, trying to remain professional. "I did, and the answer is still going to have to be no."

"I don't take no for an answer, Ms. Charcoal. I get what I

want." Turning, he dismissed anything else I might have said.

Bart's ripped pants blew in the breeze, and the way he winced slightly with each step, was almost my undoing. He was forced to walk past guests who gawked curiously at the full moon shining from the gaping hole in his pants and underwear.

When he disappeared inside the museum, I turned to Jack with a grin. "Suli really took him down a peg."

"I'm pretty sure getting pegged wasn't on his to-do list today. Or ever," Jack snickered. Wrapping his arm around my waist, he gave me a tight side-hug. "Only two more hours, and we can head back to the hotel, Firefly."

"That sounds amazing," I groaned. "My feet are killing me, and I'd love a long soak in the tub."

"If you keep groaning like that, I'm not sure we'll make it to the end of the day," Jack teased, leaning down to give me a quick kiss on the lips.

Suli blew out a long-suffering sigh and tried to cover her eyes with her massive foot. *I don't want to see you two start mating. I've seen enough of that on the television since awakening. Also, why do humans pretend they don't have breeding needs, but then record themselves breeding to entice others to breed?*

I rubbed my temple, feeling a headache coming on. *That's it! When we get back to the hotel, I'm putting child safety on your television.*

Have you forgotten I'm far older than you? I don't need to be guarded. Do you know how many orgies—

Stop! Whatever you're about to tell me, I'm not ready to hear it, I pleaded.

Sulseti cracked open one eye to study me. *You're right. Maybe when you are a few decades older, I can teach you some things...*

What had my grandmother been smoking when she decided to bind this crazy chick to me?

That you're boring, Suli cackled.

Standing, she ambled away to the far side of the fence and ignored me.

A group of children ran up to the fence, and Jack drifted into the crowd, giving me space to work with the children who'd just entered the gardens.

With the hilarious image of Bart's horrified face as Suli stuck it to him firmly fixed in my mind, the rest of the workday flew by.

CHAPTER FIFTEEN
-ARIZONA-

Why can't a T-Rex clap?
BECAUSE THEY'RE DEAD.

"I don't know, you guys. I'm telling you! Bartholomew is about to make a move." Chewing my lip, I rubbed the nylon of Albert's leash between my fingers as we walked.

It was a beautiful morning for a walk. Rez, Zon, and Suli had shifted before I'd opened the warehouse door. Now Jack and I walked down the quiet backstreet, boxed between Rez and Zon, with Suli trotting behind us.

"You don't need to worry; we've got your back." Reaching out, Jack squeezed my hand.

And such a great backside it is. No wonder your mates can't keep their hands off—

"Enough, Suli!" But I laughed.

What did she say? Zonkut asked, eyeing the triceratops.

She was complimenting my derriere and joking about how you two can't keep your hands to yourself.

Zon slowed his steps, checking out my posterior. *I agree with Suli; it is fantastic.* His tongue lolled out of his mouth, and he panted playfully.

Suli fake gagged. *Seriously? Can't he go a few hours without trying to get in your pants?*

"You don't need to worry, Ari. I'm watching every visitor who seems the slightest bit suspicious," Jack tried to reassure me. "If anyone catches my eye, I give Rez and Zon a cue, and they keep an eye on the visitor until they leave."

"I know that. And the museum staff have followed our restrictions down to the letter. But I can feel it in my bones, Jack. Bartholomew is going to do something." How could I explain what I was sensing when I barely understood it myself?

"Bart tried to make a move, and got a horn shoved up his backdoor for his trouble." Jack coughed, failing to hide his chuckle.

None of my men had been happy about Bartholomew's dismissiveness when I'd told him I was taken. But the shock and hilarity of Suli's actions had taken most of the fire from their fury.

Suli was good about making herself scarce so I could enjoy downtime with my mates. Still, it would take time for us to get comfortable sharing our space with another person. But her actions with Barty-Boy yesterday had earned Rez and Zon's respect, and they'd been less standoffish since.

144

What are you feeling, my queen? Rez's gentle voice rumbled in my mind.

Of course, my gentle giant would be the one to care about my feelings, instead of focusing on the irrationality of my worries. "I can't explain it, Rez. I can't hear his thoughts, so I don't have concrete proof."

Tears burned the back of my eyes, and my nose twitched. "But every time he stops by to speak with Teresa, I can almost taste the sourness of his greed in the air. I know people see him as a powerful businessman who knows how to make things happen... but there is something off about him."

Then we will watch him closer. Today is the last day. Tomorrow morning, we can head home. Rez tried to calm my fraying nerves. Bowing his massive head, he tenderly nuzzled me.

Wiping away a stray tear, I pressed a kiss to his skin. "Thanks. I know I'm probably worrying over nothing, but I can't help it. There's no way I could forgive myself if he kidnapped any of you."

I'd spoken out loud, and all three dinosaurs trilled in amusement.

"What are you laughing at?" I demanded.

"They're a bit big to be stolen." Jack's lips twitched as he tried to keep a straight face.

I sniffed. "A magician made the Statue of Liberty disappear, so a determined thief could steal my shifters!"

Jack sucked his cheeks in as he fought his laughter.

"Firefly, have you forgotten these dinosaurs are alive? They aren't going to allow themselves to be kidnapped."

He had a point, but I wasn't going to admit it.

"Everyone, just stay alert, okay? It will make me feel better," I pleaded.

We'll happily do whatever floats your goat. The raptor's long claws tapped the ground, enjoying teasing me.

It's a boat, and you know it, Zon, I grumbled good-naturedly.

Maybe the goat is on the boat. Technically, that would mean it's also floating your goat. Zon released a rumbling purr I thought was laughter, as his raptor hopped around me.

What's gotten into you? I squinted in suspicion.

The raptor happily chirped his strange bird sounds. *Nothing. I'm just relaxed after a week of being able to release my beast. And I'm excited to be heading home tomorrow, where we can have you all to ourselves.*

Images of him holding onto the chains as he claimed me flashed through my mind, causing heat to blaze through my body.

You do realize I can smell you when you're horny, jeertelk? The triceratops pretended to vomit behind me. *Get a room… and preferably not the one next to mine. You have an impressive set of lungs even when you think you're being quiet—you're not.*

"Jeertelk." I sounded out the unfamiliar word.

Rez tripped, nearly face-planting on the concrete, and Zon's head snapped in my direction so fast I thought he'd break it.

"What does it mean? Is it a shifter word?" Jack asked.

"I have no idea what it means. Suli has called me by it twice. Based on context, I'm guessing it means something like an idiot."

Both my shifter mates were wheezing.

Suli's laughter exploded in my brain.

"Am I wrong? What does it mean?" I looked at Zon.

Why are you asking me? Ask someone else. The raptor refused to make eye contact.

"Fine. I will." Tilting my head back, I stared up at Rez.

Realizing I was expecting an answer from him, the T-Rex's eyes widened, and his short arms waved frantically.

It was the second most ridiculous thing I'd seen—coming second only to Albert herding them through the streets back home.

"Oh, come on!" I threw up my hands. "It can't be that bad."

You're right. My new bestie finally answered. *It means idiot.*

I threw up my hands. "Why are you all so dramatic? You could have just said that from the start."

The triceratops' gaze slid away from mine. She'd suddenly become fascinated by the uneven yellow lines on the street. *Idiotic semen slut, to be more precise. Just in case you wanted the full definition.*

I stopped, my jaw falling open, and Suli bumped into me.

What? It was meant as a term of endearment. I swear it on my horn!

"Remember, I know where you sleep," I teased, trying to seem angry.

Sure, she was a jerk for calling me that, but isn't that what friends were for? Only a real friend insulted you to your face, but would stick a horn up your enemy's butt for even looking at you funny.

Arriving at the museum a few minutes later, Jack led the shifters to their designated enclosures.

"Come here, Albert." I kneeled on the concrete, gently tugging him to me.

Pulling a tiny vest from my backpack, I held it up in front of him. Albert took one look at the yellow polka-dotted sweater emblazoned with the words 'Tiny Dino in Training' and tried to bolt for the exit.

"Stop acting like a diva. The hotel staff insisted on cleaning our rooms today, so I couldn't leave you alone. Hotel policies. Plus, now everyone will know you're part of the team!"

It took a lot of effort to get the tiny pig into his work uniform. By the time I finished, I was completely out of breath. Albert shook like a dog coming in from the rain, then he stiffened and stared at the garment.

"Let's go make sure everything is ready for the visitors." Standing, I moved to walk into the garden area, only to have Albert sit back on his haunches. I'd never seen a pig glare like he was at that moment, and it was the cutest thing I'd ever seen.

Ignoring his protests, I scooped him into my arms and

covered him in kisses. "Who's the cutest piglet in the world? That's right! You are!"

It is amazing how well she has tamed the spirit, Zon whispered to Rez through our shared bond.

Our mate is a powerful Vazi. It is incredible that she is able to keep the creature in her home without facing constant issues from him, Rez agreed, both men ignoring the fact that I could hear them.

With Albert in my arms, I strolled over to the section of fence nearest my raptor mate. "You know one day you'll have to accept that he is part of our family."

These creatures do not have a family. They are solitary spirits who occasionally come together to create mammoth-scale catastrophes for their personal amusement, Zon retorted, while releasing a string of clicks.

"Albert is a pig. An animal. My pet. That's all." I rolled my eyes at his nonsense.

But somewhere deep in my mind, a seed of doubt had begun to grow.

That's what he wants you to believe, Zon growled in my mind. *And he must want you to believe it pretty badly to be willing to wear that ancient-awful sweater.*

Albert grunted and glanced up at me as if to say, 'See? I told ya it was fugly.'

Except that had to be a trick of the light, didn't it? Albert couldn't read my mind, so he couldn't know that Zon was insulting his fashion sense.

You forced the creature to wear that monstrosity. It is your fashion sense—not his—that is lacking, Zon corrected.

Albert sniffed, and I reminded myself for the hundredth time that I was just being paranoid thanks to Bartholomew's skulking around the past week.

He's just a pig. He's just a pig, I repeated.

Hmpf. The raptor shook his head before wandering off to greet the first group of visitors for the day.

"Oh! My backpack!" I'd forgotten to pick it back up after dressing Albert.

Spinning on my heel, I hurried back toward the alcove near the entrance. The backpack leaned against the wall where I'd left it, but there was a man rifling through the contents.

"Hey! That's mine!" I called out.

The man yanked his hand out of the pocket as though a viper had just bitten him. "Oh. I was... was..." He stumbled over his words. "Trying to find some type of ID so I could look for the owner."

He shoved the bag into my arms, refusing to make eye contact. It took me a second, but then I recognized him as one of the gardeners.

"Hmm. Thank you." I didn't trust his words, but I didn't really have a good reason to doubt him, either.

It was completely logical to find an ID and use it to locate the owner, but why had he looked so guilty when I'd caught his hand in the bag?

Without another word, the guy rushed away.

"Just one more day. You only have to keep it together for one more freaking day," I muttered to myself.

The sooner we got far, far away from Bartholomew, the

sooner I could stop being so paranoid. If I wasn't careful, I was going to start talking about how aliens from a planet with a weird name like Relkoi were real and were abducting people on Earth. Heck, I might even start believing the government really was putting the fluoride in toothpaste in order to track people from outer space.

It was a slippery slope when you started believing everything was a conspiracy... and I slept with dinosaur shifters, and believed in magic, so it wasn't like I was starting with a completely stable foundation to begin with.

At least you're pretty. Suli broke into my discombobulated thoughts.

She really needed to study up on how pep talks were supposed to work.

And yet, you're smiling, she gloated.

Whatever, I huffed.

With Albert tucked under my arm, I began making my rounds through the park, talking with guests, and handing out dinosaur stickers to the kids. After a few hours, my worries dissipated, and I began to have fun.

It really was entertaining to watch how the kids reacted to the dinosaurs. If it hadn't been for the stress Bartholomew had created for us during the trip, I might have enjoyed putting on events like this more often.

The ground trembled as Rez made his way to where I stood, surrounded by a sea of summer camp kids. Lowering his head, he nuzzled me. *If you would like to do this again in the future, we wouldn't mind. I've enjoyed being shifted, and my beast is happy to not have to hide.*

Rez finished speaking and licked me.

"Ack!" I screamed, trying to brush my sticky hair back down.

The kids around me dissolved into giggles, and the more I tried to fix my hair, the harder they laughed.

"You're making it worse, Miss Arizona." A pigtailed sweetheart wrapped her arms around her belly as she laughed.

"Yeah. It's sticking up like you forgot to brush it this morning," a tiny boy with a heavy dusting of freckles added.

Giving me a smile, the camp instructor led the kids away to visit Suli one final time before the camp ended.

My heart melted a bit as I watched them approach her enclosure. As soon as Suli spotted the kids, she began hopping around, wiggling her butt, and putting on a show for her tiny fans.

I had to hand it to Sulseti. She'd adjusted to the modern world far faster than I'd thought possible. Sure, she had a lot more to learn, but she was taking everything in stride. And she'd stopped growling at dogs, and eating food from the trash cans, so I definitely called that progress.

A movement in my peripheral vision caught my attention.

A gardener I didn't recognize had crossed the fence and entered Zonkut's enclosure. The raptor was lying down, taking a nap while he sunbathed in the Texas heat.

The man stealthily crept toward the resting raptor.

Zon! Wake up! I screamed into our link.

Don't stress, babe. I knew he was here before he even crossed the fence. Zon's words held amusement, not anger or fear.

Why didn't you call for me? I would have stopped him.

And spoil my fun? No way. Now watch this... Zon's voice faded from the link just as the man stepped close enough to touch him.

My panic was reaching a boiling point. This broke the terms of the agreement. No one other than myself, or one of my personal team, was to cross the fence into the dinosaurs' exhibits.

The guys were right.

I shouldn't have worried.

CHAPTER SIXTEEN
-ARIZONA-

Why should you never ask a dinosaur
to read you a story?
BECAUSE THEIR TALES ARE SO LONG.

Zon moved with the speed of an apex predator. Smoothly spinning around, his tail knocked the man off his feet. The guy hadn't even hit the grass before Zon leaped forward, using one of his long, taloned feet to pin the man beneath him.

Leaning down, the raptor snapped his jaws in the man's pale, terror -stricken face.

He wet his pants, Zon snickered into the shared bond. *Maybe I should give him a little nibble? So he has something to remember me by?*

Bad Raptor! Back away, I ordered in the bond, as if I could actually control one of the fiercest predators to walk the earth. *Believe me, he will never forget you. This guy is going to spend the next ten years dreaming about you every single night.*

The raptor hissed down at the trespasser one final time before reluctantly releasing him. Zon's eyes locked on me hurrying toward him and raced to my side with a self-satisfied trill.

Giving him a quick pat, I focused my building fury on the man trying to stay upright on his wobbly noodle legs.

I wasted no time. "What are you doing in here?"

"No-nothing," the guy lied, the whites of his eyes showing as Zon moved to stand behind me.

Jack ran up to the fence. "What's going on? Is everything okay?"

"I'm just about to find that out," I growled. "Go get Teresa."

Jack hesitated for the briefest of moments before hurrying away.

Thinking I was distracted, the guy bent and snatched something from the dirt. He quickly stuffed it in his pocket.

"What was that?" I snapped, stalking toward him.

"Just my phone. It must have fallen from my pocket."

He was lying to my face, and I wasn't going to have it.

"Show me." I held out my hand, but the guy stuck his hands in his pocket and took a step back.

"Listen. You do not want to try my patience. What did you pick up?" I repeated, taking another step forward.

The man looked like he was about to pass out from fear. Not from me, but from the crouching raptor tiptoeing behind me like a cartoon cat sneaking up on a mouse.

Monsieur Pee Pants took another step back.

I was close enough to make out the name written on his

nametag. "John Smith? That's your name? You've got to be kidding me."

Why didn't he just wear a tag that said, 'Hi, I'm a spy.'

Jack returned to the fence with Teresa hot on his heels.

"John! What are you doing in there? You know the rules of working in the exhibits," Teresa panted, trying to catch her breath.

"The speaker system in this area has been acting up, and I thought I saw some exposed wires. I didn't want the robot to trip and the museum be blamed if he was damaged." John rattled off the excuse with a practiced smoothness.

More lies, Zon hissed. *Those blasted speakers have worked fine all week. I wish they'd break so I wouldn't have to listen to the loop of animal calls. Those creatures didn't even exist in my day.*

"If there was an issue, it should've been addressed after the dinosaurs were removed for the day. If it needed immediate attention, you were supposed to take the matter to Arizona." Teresa pinched the bridge of her nose, her chest heaving. "You do realize this breached the contract we signed with Dinovation, right? They could press charges for this."

She wasn't wrong. The contract we'd signed was explicitly clear that during exhibit hours, the area inside the dinosaur exhibits was considered private property solely controlled by Dinovation. It had been one of our stipulations before signing, specifically to prevent things like the current situation.

"I'm sorry, ma'am. I wasn't thinking. The raptor seemed

to be in sleep mode, and I thought I could check it out real quick. But no harm, no foul."

"Then why did you creep up on the raptor instead of immediately heading for the speakers?" Crossing my arms, I waited for him to spew more lies.

John eased toward the fence, trying to get away from Zon and me... Fine, mostly Zon.

"Stop. I want to see what you stuffed in your pocket." I stepped so close our noses almost touched, then I smelled his urine and took a step back.

"I already told you, lady! It's just my phone." He unconsciously moved to cover the object in his pocket.

"Then show me." Holding out my hand, I waited for Mister Lost-My-Balls to prove he was telling the truth.

"It's private property. You can't make me," he spat.

Bold words for a guy standing three feet from a raptor who would eagerly rip the head from his body if I said the word. I guess I was wrong. His nutsack wasn't empty— probably shriveled—but not nutless.

Crossing my arms over my chest, I rolled my eyes. "I have a six-hundred-pound dino at my back that says otherwise. Quit messing around and pull it out."

I bet he's been waiting his whole life for a girl to say that to him.

Shut up, Suli. I'm trying to look scary.

Hold up! Is that your intimidation face? Girl, you look like you're disappointed he didn't make a happy plate at dinner. It's a good thing you have three shifters for protection, because I've seen human kids scarier than you. Do you want me to send one of the scouts over to kick his legs for you?

My grandmother must have been high on Mesozoic Era mushrooms when she decided Suli would be a great gift.

It's possible. The priestess was a cool woman, with a killer sense of humor.

Blocking Suli from my mind, I wiggled my fingers at the gardener. "Today, preferably."

"No." John straightened his spine. "I know my rights."

Never taking my eyes from John's craggy, weather-worn face, I called out, "Jack?"

Jack effortlessly hopped over the fence and headed straight for John.

The gardener watched his approach with curiosity that quickly turned to shock when Jack pulled a set of silver cuffs from the pocket of his tactical pants.

"Hey, man! You can't do that." John jerked away from Jack's grip on his arm. "Ms. Teresa, tell them they have no right to do this."

"I take it you didn't read the employment agreement we required all employees to sign before working this event?" Teresa rubbed her forehead. "If you had, you would remember the clause that explained Dinovation and their security officer had the right to search, confiscate, question, and file charges against any employee who breached the agreement and entered the enclosures while a dinosaur was inside."

Sighing heavily, she added, "I can call an attorney for

you, but they won't be able to stop Dinovation from acting on their rights. The contract is solid."

"I can't afford an attorney! The job didn't pay that well," John shouted, the veins in his thick neck throbbing.

There was something about the way he said *job* that caught my interest. Something about it seemed like he wasn't talking about his employment as a gardener. Magic began to smolder in my chest, reminding me I needed to keep my emotions in check.

Teresa was glancing anxiously around at the guests, who were beginning to realize drama was going down in the raptor pen.

Not wanting John's actions to take away from the hard work Teresa had done bringing the summer camp together, I stepped close to him and whispered, "John, we are going to take this inside. Either you walk with us and don't create a fuss, or I will have Jack forcibly cuff you. Your choice."

"I'll walk with you," John snarled.

"Then let's go," Jack ordered, his tone made of steel.

While Jack was harsh, he was surprisedly courteous as he opened the gate and motioned for John to walk through ahead of us.

As we passed Teresa, I dropped my voice low so anyone nearby wouldn't overhear. "With only a few hours left of the program, I don't want the attention on this mess. Can we use one of the meeting rooms to talk to John? And are you willing to sit in on the conversation as a witness?"

I wasn't an idiot. We were acting within our rights, but the world was sue-happy, and I wasn't going to risk a 'he said, she said' situation in the future if this became a legal matter.

"Absolutely!" The tension in Teresa's face eased, and she sighed in relief. "And thank you. We've worked so hard on this, and I can see someone deciding to run a news story over this rather than the good the camp did for the kids. Drama sells."

She led us into a small meeting room with a single window looking out on the museum's gardens.

"Don't worry, these windows are mirrored. No one can see in," Teresa assured us.

Halley's Comet! Did she think we were going to torture John for answers and wouldn't want to risk witnesses?

"Thank you, Teresa." Jack pulled a seat out for her to sit in and quickly did the same for me.

Then his demeanor shifted in front of our eyes, going from an easy-going gentleman to a stony-eyed security officer. "Empty your pockets onto the table."

"No." John curled his lip in disgust.

"Please, place all the items from your pockets on the table. I will not ask again," Jack repeated. His icy, calm voice nearly had me wanting to dump my own pockets out on the table.

I sat Albert on the floor. Since the door was shut, I figured he could enjoy stretching his legs while we questioned John.

My magic popped and crackled like embers in a fire. I'd been doing well to keep my emotions under control to keep my magic from wreaking havoc.

It was exhausting having a campfire inside me that needed constant tending to ensure it stayed inside the stone barrier surrounding it. A single wrong move, and the cozy campfire could turn into a forest fire that devoured everything in its path.

This wasn't how I wanted our last hours at the museum to go. I was tired, my feet ached, a migraine was building at the back of my skull, and my magic was growing restless.

I wanted John to just follow the simple command.

"Put everything in your pockets on the table." My words were flat and unemotional, but they carried the persuasive power of my magic.

John's mind bent to my request, forcing his hands to obey the order.

Jack shot me an unreadable expression, probably suspecting I'd used magic.

As the contents of John's pockets clattered onto the table, I spotted the item he'd grabbed off the ground and tried to conceal from me.

"Well, it's definitely not a phone," I stated the obvious, leaning in to get a better look at the rectangular device.

There were spiderweb cracks spread across the tiny screen, and one of its plastic corners had broken off.

"What is it?" I hadn't intended to weave a magic command into my question, but to my surprise, John answered.

"It's an E-Reader."

"You want me to believe you were going to read the

raptor a naptime story?" I lifted an eyebrow. I wasn't as old as Rez, but I hadn't been born yesterday, either.

Jack's low, husky chuckle had my magic unfurling a bit more, thanks to the fated mate bond and the constant pull I felt toward him. I could admit it. I was obsessed with my mates.

With the fresh surge of magic, my fingertips began to tingle. Worried I might start shooting sparks, I clasped my hands together under the table.

"It's a hacking device. It reads electronic signals and finds a way to infiltrate the computer system to mine data." Jack's eyes locked on John's face. "Correct?"

Since Jack's order didn't come with a side serving of my freaky power of suggestion, John didn't respond. Instead, John stupidly tried to stare Jack down... but eventually caved as his eyes slid from Jack's intense gaze.

"I'll take that as a yes." My mate rubbed his jaw.

John had intended to steal our technology. My muscles twitched as I fought my emotions.

"I didn't use it, but I couldn't even if I wanted to. The device doesn't work," John grumbled. "Freaking waste of time."

"How do you know it doesn't work if you didn't use it?" Jack leaned toward John, forcing the slightly smaller man to ease back in his chair.

"It was working when I was holding it near my phone this morning. As soon as I entered the raptor exhibit, it stopped working and didn't pick up any electronic signals."

"So you would have used it if it hadn't malfunctioned." My magic surged with my rage, sending tendrils of magic tumbling over the barrier keeping the power contained. It wasn't a flood... not yet. But I was definitely beginning to leak.

Arizona, are you okay? Where are you? Rez sounded worried.

Still interviewing the wannabe spy. I'm— I hesitated, wanting to lie so I could reassure them, but I couldn't lie to my mates. *I'm struggling with my magic, but I'm handling it.*

Ari, your magic goes from zero to sixty faster than a hummingbird's heart can take a beat. You need to get out of there and away from anything setting you off before you blow up another museum. I'll shift and come to you. Zonkut was ready to risk everything for me.

No! I protested. *If you do that, all our work to keep you guys a secret will have been for nothing. I'm handling it better than I did at the restaurant.*

And I'm proud of you, darling. But you have also grown more powerful since then, which means a slip could create more devastation. Rez's words brushed against my mind in a gentle caress.

Let us try and get our answers, please. I can do this, I pleaded. We were so close.

We know you can, little queen. But that won't keep us from worrying. There is nothing more precious to us than you. Rez's belief in me caused my heart to swell with pride.

Jack had continued questioning John while I'd been

dealing with my shifter mates' concerns, but skilled as he was, John wasn't giving much information up.

Sweat trickled down my spine, and my hair grew damp. The room was heating up, or maybe it was my temperature that was rising?

"John." I steadied my voice, masking the strain I was under as more of my magic spilled over the barrier. "Who hired you to use the device?"

"I don't know." John met my gaze, his bloodshot eyes flickering between hate and confusion as he answered each of my questions honestly.

My heart began to flutter erratically in my chest as magic rippled through me. A reminder of the bigger wave that was coming.

Keep it together, Arizona, I coached myself, concentrating on strengthening the containment field around my power. A couple more questions… that's all I needed.

"Fine. Who gave you the device? And what were you supposed to do with it once you collected the information they wanted?"

Each time I used my magic to press him to answer me, my magic grew in size, making it harder to control. My body began to vibrate.

Ari, Zon warned. *I can sense the spike in your magic.*

Two more minutes, I responded breathlessly.

"Some kid… never seen…" John was spilling the tea, but I could barely hear him over the roar of magic-charged blood pumping through my veins.

Someone had nearly found out my dinosaurs were real.

That would have jeopardized their safety and gotten them taken from me. I was getting more furious with each passing minute. I tried to breathe slow and steady through my nose, but my respiration had been reduced to jerky pants.

Focus, Ari, I ordered myself. *Get the info and get out of this room.*

"Okay, so you didn't recognize him, and he didn't give you his name. Then how were you supposed to give the equipment back afterward?" Jack prodded.

"The kid gave me a key to a storage locker on the edge of town. I was supposed to leave the E-Reader there after work tonight," John answered, his eyes remaining locked on me, still under the thrall of my magic.

Look down.

Huh? Where had that come from?

Eyes... glowing...

It sounded like the masculine voice was coming through a broken vintage radio.

Don't make eye contact. The voice was slightly clearer this time. *Raise... suspicions...*

And the signal—like my childhood ability to eat junk food without gaining weight—vanished.

Was I picking up on Jack's thoughts? He was completely human, but could my magic, combined with the mate bond, make it possible? I could hear his thoughts when I focused hard enough, so maybe my magic sensed he needed to relay a message?

Glancing up, my suspicions were confirmed when I

found Jack staring hard at me. 'Your eyes,' he mouthed, giving me a discrete hand gesture to look down.

Mystery voice identified, I dropped my gaze to the granite tabletop. My body had begun to ache like I was coming down with a fever, and each time I blinked, it felt like sandpaper was scratching my lenses.

It's because you are holding in the magic without releasing it! Zon roared. *Get out, or I will shift and deal with the consequences later.*

The magic is hungry and blazing hot. It is burning through your energy reserves, and the increased temperature and profuse sweating are causing you to dehydrate incredibly fast. Rez's voice was gentler. *I don't want to do anything rash, but you have to get out of there, or we are coming in to get you.*

Why did they think they could boss me around? Already exhausted, which made me cranky, my temper flared. That's when I caught sight of the pink sparks falling from my hands.

"Do you smell that? Like crème brûlée? Or s'mores?" John sucked in a lungful of the magic-scented air and moaned. "I'd kill to have a piece of whatever that is. I've never craved anything so badly—"

Albert bit my ankle at the same time all three shifters screamed, *GET OUT!* into my brain.

"Jack, finish here, please." I kept my eyes glued to the floor as I dashed from the conference room and down the hall.

It was imperative I found somewhere I could be alone while I tried to deal with my magical meltdown. I couldn't go outside and risk the kids, but I didn't think I could contain the magic long enough to get away from the museum's visitors.

Darting down another hall, I was relieved when the sound of chatter faded away. I was putting space between me and anyone I could hurt—or accidentally seduce.

A full body shudder racked my body at the memory of John's hungry moan. That man had a better chance of getting bitten by a unicorn than he had of getting a chance to put his sour cream in my burrito.

Ew.

CHAPTER SEVENTEEN
-ARIZONA-

What would happen if a 100-ton Brachiosaurus stepped on you?
YOU'D BE DEEPLY IMPRESSED.

T he hall I was in must have been under construction, because the rooms were unfinished and bare of standard office decor. Finding a darkened doorway to my left that wasn't blocked off by tape, ladders, or various tools, I darted inside.

Slamming the door behind me, I flicked the lock and allowed myself to collapse to my knees on the floor. I wrapped my arms around my middle and rocked, trying to ease the pressure that was reaching a boiling point inside me.

You have to release some of it! Rez bellowed. *Hurry!*

I can't, I whimpered. *If I drop my walls to let some magic out, I think it will all rush out.*

And if you keep it all in, you will die. Rez was distraught.

I'm scared. Tears streamed down my cheeks.

Where is Jack? Zon snarled into the link. *He better be dead, because that's the only excuse I'll accept for why he isn't with you.*

He's taking care of the situation with the gardener. I asked him to do it, I sobbed.

I could hear the tyrannosaurus's roar of frustration through the museum walls.

Ari, listen to me. Zon's voice had dropped, turning husky. *You're going to do exactly what I say. Do you understand me?*

Yes, I croaked.

That's my good girl, Zon purred.

My body, ever responsive to my mates, sent liquid heat rushing between my thighs. The dark room began to glow a soft pink as my magic turned me into a human glow stick.

I wish we could do this slow, but you need to come hard and fast. We have to siphon off some of this magic, Zon growled.

At his words, my stomach twisted itself in knots. Gasping from the pain, I doubled over.

Beautiful, I want you to close your eyes, Zon directed, giving me a moment to obey before he spoke again. *Are you wet for me?*

Yes, I whimpered.

I want you to take two fingers and slide them into that sexy lace thong you put on this morning, Zon rumbled.

My ears popped as my magic expanded, pushing hard to escape my body.

Do it now! Zon growled.

I did as he ordered, sliding my fingers inside my soaked entrance.

That's good. Zon's voice was so low it was barely intelligible. *Now stroke yourself. Pretend I'm in front of you, watching you pleasure yourself.*

My walls clenched, tightening around my fingers at the mental image of him watching me.

Zon cursed. *I'm so hard and it is not comfortable in this form. The last thing I need is one of these humans to snap a photo, so I'm lying down on the grass just to hide it.*

Knowing Zon was just as turned on by our telepathic sex was all the push I needed to begin stroking myself in earnest.

My ragged breathing turned into fast pants as I tried to find my release, but it just wouldn't come... or more accurately, I couldn't come.

How could I focus on controlling the magic while also trying to relax enough to orgasm? It was like trying to pat my head and rub my stomach at the same time.

I can't. I'm sorry, Zon.

Wrapping my arms around my middle, I bent over until my sweat-beaded forehead was pressed against the cold tiles. I sighed, savoring the brief moment of relief from the inner inferno that threatened to burn me alive.

The door to the room flew open and slammed into the wall. "Arizona!" Jack shouted in relief. "There you are. What's wrong?"

"Too much magic," I whimpered.

My skin had moved from a feverish ache to an I-fell-asleep-for-three-hours-while-sunbathing type of burn. It was pure agony.

"You're glowing." Jack closed and locked the door before kneeling in front of me. I watched my magic cast a pink glow onto his awestruck face.

I choked on a sob, unable to talk as another cramp tried to tear me in half. The edges of my vision darkened, and I was tempted to give myself over to the bliss of unconsciousness. At least I wouldn't feel anything if I passed out. But I couldn't let myself give up. The moment I did that, my magic would be free to terrorize everyone and everything in my vicinity.

"Tell me how to help you, Firefly." Jack reached for me.

"No!" I cried out, trying to scoot away from him. "I don't know what will happen to you if you touch me. You shouldn't be here. I could be radioactive for all I know."

"You sent your magic into Rez, and he survived. I'll be fine, love." Despite my protests, Jack pulled me into his arms.

This is sweet, but you are minutes away from releasing a colossal amount of magic. He needs to help you, or bring you to us so we can try to siphon some from you. Zon was practically bellowing in my mind.

He's terrified of losing you. We both are, Rez whispered, his voice broken.

I wasn't sure Jack could handle the amount of magic that might be released if I asked him to have sex with me. But the only other option was to get myself outside to the dinosaurs. And how would I explain a sparkling magical dome to bystanders? Or what if I started calling people to me like some weird land-mermaid-pied-piper?

"Jack?" I murmured. "The quickest way to siphon off some of the unstable magic is for me to climax."

His eyes widened, and he opened his mouth, but I wasn't finished.

"I've never had this much power in me, and I don't know what will happen if I lose control. It would be safer for you to get as far from here as possible."

Jack's expression tightened. "You can forget that. I'm not leaving."

"Jack! Are you listening to me? Even if we successfully disperse enough magic that I can make it back to the warehouse without blowing up half the city, I might kill you."

Isn't that how all men want to go? Suli questioned.

I ignored her.

Jack pressed a kiss to my forehead. "I'll do whatever needs to be done if it will ease your pain."

How very noble of him. Suli snorted so hard she started choking.

I continued to ignore her.

The soft brush of his lips was enough to send another pulse of magic through me, damaging the walls I had erected to confine it.

It's not the only thing about to get erected.

I was going to learn how to block my mind as soon as we got back home. That's assuming I didn't buy a farm tonight and become a root inspector.

You aren't going to die, Suli assured me. *Unless you keep talking about it instead of doing it.*

I couldn't have responded if I'd wanted to.

Jack's finger slid under my chin, tilting my head back to give him better access to my mouth. His lips captured mine in a tender kiss that quickly turned frantic.

"You smell incredible," Jack spoke the words between kisses. "And you taste just as wonderful."

"Thanks?" The word was muffled as I trailed kisses along his jawline.

"Making love to you is always mind-blowing, but there is something insanely erotic about when you are radiating magic." Jack lifted my shirt over my head and moved his hands to my bra.

"But my magic is practically forcing your body to crave sex with me." How could he not hate me for that?

"Firefly, you aren't taking my free will away. I'm not being forced to do anything. Encouraged, maybe, but I could walk away. It's like having a nice steak. The steak would taste wonderful even without seasoning, but that same steak marinated in my secret spice blend is out of this world. Your magic is an enhancement that adds a bit of spice."

"I think that was a compliment?" I giggled, then winced as my chest muscles ached.

Jack's words had eased the lingering worry I'd unintentionally forced him to want me. I still couldn't believe he'd walked away from his job without a backward glance, just to be with me. It made no sense.

That's because you don't value yourself the same way we do. You're a treasure worth giving up the entire world for, Rez's words caressed my mind.

I love you, Rez.

Rez trilled in the bond. *I love you too, my queen. Now please breed your human so we can go home. The museum closes in two hours.*

Grabbing the hem of Jack's shirt, I pushed it up, kissing and licking his exposed chest. Jack flung the shirt away, and the rest of our clothes followed.

"Ari, this room doesn't have any furniture—"

Wrapping my arms around Jack's neck, I pulled him down on top of me. My entire backside was flattened against the tiles, and it felt wonderful against my throbbing skin... almost as good as the velvety steel rod pressed against my stomach.

"Hurry, Jack," I moaned.

Jack huffed a dry laugh. "That won't be a problem. I'm probably not going to last long. I want you so bad it hurts..." He rocked his hips, sliding his length up my stomach. "But it hurts so good."

He was definitely experiencing an aphrodisiac-induced high from my magic. I refused to feel guilty about it this time.

If couples could enjoy bonding over playtime with aphrodisiac foods, various toys, and even the random food item, then there was nothing wrong with my mates occasionally wanting to experience my magic during sex.

This was something special I could offer my mates.

Jack shifted positions slightly, aligning our bodies so that when he rocked forward a second time, the head of his erection kissed my entrance.

"Don't tease me," I growled, a sense of urgency thundering like the hoofbeats of a wild stallion in my mind.

It's about time you felt some urgency, Zon complained, but so quietly I wasn't sure if I'd imagined it.

Jack gave a single thrust, sheathing himself inside me, causing my eyes to cross.

My ears popped, and I could smell nothing but the indescribable scent of ozone that warned of coming rain… and somehow also seemed to linger in the air when I used my magic. Maybe what I thought was ozone was the same as the pheromone my men had described to me?

"Jack!" My body trembled violently, and the power slammed against the last of my shields.

He didn't respond, but he began to pound into me with wild abandon. The effect on my overly stimulated body was unexpected. As Jack hammered into me, the magic stilled, distracted by our fated mate who was working a different kind of wizardry with his hips… *and magic wand.*

Not for the first time, I wished I had better control of my magic. Then instead of fighting to keep it from going supernova, I could be using it to blow Jack's mind. Of course, the last time I'd used magic during sex with him, I thought I'd killed him.

Jack's hand moved between our bodies, his finger finding the sensitive pearl in my clam. The delicious friction had my back arching off the floor. He took advantage of my bare breasts being shoved in his face and sucked my nipple into his mouth.

"Ohhh, Jack!" I moaned, as my orgasm built hard and fast.

He began eagerly alternating between lapping and sucking my breast. When his tongue started flicking my nipple in perfect unison with his finger strokes, it was my undoing.

I clenched my teeth to keep from screaming and drawing unwanted attention to our unauthorized activities. My body shook with aftershocks that were nearly as strong as the original orgasm.

When the last of the orgasms finally faded, I was surprised to discover Jack had restrained himself while I surfed the waves of delirium. The relentless pressure of the magic had vanished. It was no longer fighting to escape.

What was strange was that my magic hadn't dissipated. Jack hadn't siphoned it away like the dino shifters did when I was struggling.

I closed my eyes, focusing on my magic.

What I discovered had my eyes opening wide.

My magic was stable—at least for the moment. It was swirling beneath my skin, moving with Jack's movements.

I wonder—

Don't you dare! Zonkut's frustration seeped through the bond. *Now is not the time for experiments. Especially ones involving your feral magic.*

Ignoring him, I closed my eyes and invited my magic to come play. For a moment, nothing happened. Then the magic merged with me. We weren't fighting for control. I wasn't treating it like a curse that needed to be locked away, and in turn, the magic wasn't trying to escape a captor.

Now to test how much the magic could do.

A naughty grin spread across my face.

"Firefly?" Jack's eyebrows knit together.

Imagining the thick erection currently buried inside me, I worked to wrap the magic around his length. My magic did as I asked. When Jack thrust inside me again, I tightened the magic, gently squeezing.

"Firefly," Jack choked, his eyes widening with shock. "Are you doing that?"

"Yes. I am," I answered, voice husky.

Jack groaned as my magic moved along his length. "How?"

With effort, I was able to guide my magic to move in rhythm with the rocking of Jack's hips. I was essentially giving him a magical hand job, squeezing and rolling, while he plunged inside my heat.

"Never mind. You can do it because everything about you is unbelievable." His body trembled, and his eyes closed.

Jack was thoroughly lost in the pleasure I was giving him, and I was freaking proud of myself. There was just one more thing I wanted to try.

Drawing on the memory of the vibrations I experienced when my magic was closest to bursting free, I coaxed the playful magic to try making just one place vibrate, and not my whole body.

My magic seemed to like the idea of a challenge and rushed to complete the task.

When Jack slid out and thrust back into my heat, he didn't just experience the magical milking. This time, my slick walls, which already squeezed his erection like a glove on a hand, began to vibrate.

"Ari." Unable to put together a sentence, Jack sucked in a deep breath and released it with a hiss. "Love, oh man... I can't process... frick—" He ended the broken ramble with a deep growl that sent vibrations through both of us.

I hadn't thought human men could growl, but it turned out I was wonderfully mistaken.

Jack's strokes grew slower with each thrust, and his breathing turned to shallow rasps.

"I can't last any longer," he grunted, pumping into me twice more before his body stiffened, and while his length jerked, my magic continued to draw out every last bit of pleasure.

When he collapsed on top of me, we were both exhausted. I could have fallen asleep right there on the hard floor and slept like a rock.

The air still carried a hint of magic, but most of it was lazily moving in my body like lava in a lava lamp.

My magic and I had a long way to go, but this had been a promising first training session. I was learning a lot as I went along, since it wasn't like I had a Vazi I could ask for advice.

But I was getting the impression that working with magic was like training a dog to perform tricks and tasks.

With each session, the trainer made sure the tricks were engaging, which taught the dog that working with the trainer was fun.

I had a lot of training to do, but I finally had an idea of how to start.

CHAPTER EIGHTEEN
-ARIZONA-

A new study claims dinosaurs didn't go extinct from the comet.
IT WAS CAUSED BY REPTILE DYSFUNCTION.

As I caught my breath and the fog cleared from my brain, the real world came into sharp focus.

"Jack!" I pushed him off me and sat up. "Who's watching the dinos? What happened to John? Where is Albert?"

"You forgot when." Sitting up, Jack stretched his arms over his head and rolled his shoulders.

"What?" He was making no sense.

Jack gave me a lazy smile. "You asked who, what, and where, but you skipped when."

I blinked.

Jack leaned in and kissed the tip of my nose. "Stop worrying. I know a few people at the local police station, and one of the guys picked John up. They wanted to finger-print him and check for any outstanding warrants."

Standing, Jack began searching for our clothes that he'd yeeted all over the room. With my uranium-flavored gummy-worm glow gone, the room was only dimly lit by a light Jack must have flipped on when he entered the room.

"The dinos are ancient. I'm pretty sure they can watch themselves while you work on not becoming a human Roman candle. Plus, Teresa was on high alert. No one would dare step within a meter of the fences." Jack pulled on his pants and shirt, and I fought the ridiculous urge to pout.

I was beginning to think I preferred my men barefoot and prehistoric.

Suli giggled in appreciation of my word play. *Except Jack isn't a dinosaur or prehistoric.*

Okay, fine. How about this? I like my men barefoot and packing.

Better. Except do you only want them barefooted, or naked all over? Don't tell me you have a foot fetish. Erghhh. Suli added gagging sounds to really emphasize her opinion.

You aren't supposed to yuck other peoples' yums, I chided. *But yeah, feet are gross. Hang on… how do you know about a foot fetish? Or fetishes at all, for that matter?*

Jack gave me a tablet and earbuds a few nights ago. Suli's excitement nearly bubbled over. *I found this application where people post videos on all kinds of topics. It's been great to learn how humans really speak every day. Slang in this era is lit!*

That was nice of Jack. It was a sweet gesture, but I

wondered if he'd just opened a dino-sized can of worms by giving Suli online access.

Apparently, he didn't want me to feel uncomfortable with the way you guys make your bedrock during tyrannosaurus sex, while playing with your human and two bonersaurus shifters. Suli kept it together until the end, then she dissolved into a fit of laughter.

My mouth hung open as I tried to process the way she had roasted me, and tried to decide if I should be humiliated or amused.

Definitely not humiliated. Sex and breeding are normal… and fun. The last orgy I went to had over thirty—

NOT LISTENING! I cut her off. *I'm not old enough to know that stuff yet, remember?*

Whatever. Get dressed and let's get out of here.

"Earth to Arizona." Jack held my bra, thong, and pants in his outstretched hand. His lips twisted in a smirk and one eyebrow was raised.

Blushing, I took the garments. "How long have you been waiting for me to take those?"

"Two or three minutes, I'd say. But it looked like you were enjoying the conversation, so it's no big deal."

"It was Suli. She's taken to working puns into conversations now. Some of them are kinda funny." I hurriedly dressed. "Where is Albert? With Teresa?"

"No, I brought him with me when I started searching for you. He led me to you. He's in here somewhere." Jack's eyes scanned the room.

"Ah-ha!" He strode to one corner and lifted my shirt from the floor, revealing a sleeping pig.

I was relieved he wasn't wandering around the museum or in the gardens terrorizing the dinosaurs, but it was weird knowing he might've watched the whole thing. At least when Rez had claimed me on the beach, Albert had been too busy chasing crabs and seagulls to acknowledge us.

"Looks like he's been snoozing." Jack leaned down, scratching Albert's favorite spot behind his ears.

I walked to Jack's side, taking my shirt from his hand and quickly pulling it over my head. Once I'd smoothed it in place, I bent and gathered Albert in my arms.

"Did you have a nice nap, buddy?" I cooed.

Albert stared up at me with innocent eyes, before cuddling into my arms and yawning.

"Looks like he is still exhausted." I kissed the top of his head.

Jack pulled his phone from his pocket and glanced at the screen. The museum closed in less than two hours, then we could head home.

All I wanted was a shower and to sleep for a week, but I kept my agreements, and I wasn't a whiner, so I pasted a smile on my face. "Let's do this!"

You know that kind of silliness won't work on us, Zon teased. *And I doubt it would have worked on Jack if he hadn't been tired from the past week as well. Not much gets by him.*

Jack opened the door, and we made our way down the hall, with his hand resting on the small of my back. When we pushed through the heavy glass doors, the late afternoon sunshine nearly blinded me.

We made our way to each enclosure, checking that no one was harassing the dinos. Jack was right; the staff was giving the enclosures a wide berth.

A soft buzz came from Jack's pocket. He pulled out his phone, saw the name, and excused himself to take the call away from the people milling around us.

"Well, I guess it's just us now, Albert," I murmured, smiling when he affectionately rubbed his cheek against my shirt.

Making my way to the small lockers in one of the museum's alcoves, I typed my code and pulled out my backpack. Rummaging through it, I pulled out my water bottle, as well as the smaller water bottle I carried for Albert, and a collapsible dog bowl.

Lifting my bottle to my dry lips, I chugged the water. I found myself unable to stop until I'd drunk all but about an inch in the bottom of the bottle. The shifters had been right about my magic dehydrating me.

When Albert finished his drink, I put our things away and headed toward Suli's enclosure where a group of kids had gathered. My legs were still wobbly, and my head ached, but I could push through.

I spent the next twenty minutes moving between exhibits, answering questions, and letting people pet or take selfies with Albert. He seemed to eat up the attention.

When the family I'd been speaking to moved to another part of the garden, I sagged onto a bench. My head fell back against the back of the chair, suddenly too heavy for my neck to support.

"There you are, beautiful!" Jack sat down beside me, putting his arm around my shoulders so that my head now rested against his arm rather than on the hard back of the bench.

"Hi there." I was surprised at how much effort it was taking to put together a sentence.

Fatigue from my near magic burnout was hitting me hard. I didn't know if I'd ever been this tired before. How was I going to make it another hour and a half?

Tell Jack, Rez encouraged. *He's your mate, he deserves to know.*

I'd been on my own for so long that it was hard to admit when I was struggling. But Rez was right. I needed to learn to ask for help.

"Jack? I'm not feeling great. I'm so tired I don't think I can walk another step, or answer another question. My brain is foggy, making it hard to concentrate. I think I need to drink a gallon of water and sleep." I looked anywhere but at him as I spoke, still feeling ashamed for being weak.

"Sweetheart! Why didn't you say something sooner?" Jack pulled his phone from his pocket and tapped open the rideshare app. "Let me order you a ride. You can go on back to the hotel and rest. I can handle the last few guests and get Rez, Suli and Zon back to the warehouse so they can shift."

He tapped a few times, selecting my ride, before standing and scooping me into his arms.

"Jack! I can walk!"

"I know you can, but why should you when I'm here and love any reason to hold you?" Jack nuzzled my neck. "We'll get some to-go food and bring it back to the hotel. That way, you don't have to worry about anything but sleeping until we get there."

I rested my head against his shoulder. My mates made me feel so incredibly loved.

"Do you want me to come with you, Firefly? I could get you to the room and then come straight back here," Jack offered, as my ride turned onto the cobblestone pavement leading up to the museum's entrance.

"Don't be silly. I can get myself from the car to our room. Besides, I wouldn't be able to rest if we left the three shifters alone. Who knows what might happen?" I patted his cheek.

You guys better behave while I'm gone, I thought to Rez and Zon.

Zon huffed. *We've handled ourselves fine this week.*

He was right. I'd been proud of how unfazed the shifters had been with all the stimuli from people, vehicles, tools, and the countless other things that might have freaked them out when they'd first shifted.

You guys are amazing.

Jack ducked his head and settled me onto the car's back-seat. Batting away my hands, he buckled me in, then stole a kiss before shutting the door.

I'll see you in just over an hour. If someone annoys you, try not to peg them. Let Jack deal with them.

Suli gasped. *I'm offended you don't trust me.* Then her voice turned serious. *Don't worry about us. We've got this. Go rest. Your body needs it.*

I glanced at the driver's GPS display. It showed that with the current traffic, it would take about twenty minutes to get to the hotel.

My eyelids were too heavy to keep open. "I'm going to take a quick catnap, Albert. Don't start trouble while I'm sleeping, okay?"

Unable to resist the call of sleep any longer, I dropped my head back against the seat and was asleep before the driver had even turned onto the main street.

"Is she out cold?" a gruff voice asked.

"Yeah, man. The ex-cop stuck her in the car, and she was asleep before I pulled out of the parking lot and didn't move a muscle the whole trip. I thought she might be dead," a nasally male voice responded.

The first male gave a low whistle. "The boss ain't going to be happy. He wanted her slightly woozy, so she'd be easier to manipulate. He can't talk to her if she's unconscious. How much did you put in her drink?"

There was a long pause before the second male responded. "It was an accident, man. She left her backpack unattended, and I thought it would be easy to dose her water right then, rather than trying to find an excuse to work on the lockers. Tough Tits Teresa has been watching everyone like a hawk this week, and I wasn't sure she'd agree to let me work on the lockers while her special guests were using them."

Why couldn't I open my eyes? My brain seemed disconnected from the rest of me, and every command I gave the various parts of my body was ignored.

The first guy gave a long smoker's cough, then repeated his previous question. "So how much did you give her? She's skinny, so it wouldn't take much to make her tipsy."

"The whole thing," the second guy mumbled.

I still hadn't figured out what they were talking about. But it sounded like that poor chick was in for a rough hangover—assuming she wasn't currently in a morgue being basted in formaldehyde. Somebody should warn her.

"The whole dose?! Are you crazy? The boss is going to lose it. He doesn't want any dead bodies on his hands."

"I know, bro! It's not like I did it on purpose."

My eyes would have rolled so hard they'd have gotten stuck if I wasn't giving an Oscar-worthy performance of an inanimate doll—or a dead body. I'd always thought it might be fun to play a dead body in a movie.

My brain slowly started putting pieces together.

Great Caesar's ghost!

It was me. *I was the girl.*

And it sounded like I was about to be the proud owner of a brand-new pine condo, in one of those gated communities people were literally dying to get into. I hoped I got nice neighbors, not the kind who skulked around and refused to leave until you finally cursed them out. As long as they weren't absolute ghouls, I could get along with them.

The first man gave a humorless bark of laughter. "Boss ain't going to care if you did it on purpose or not."

"Her bottle had a cap covering a wide hole so you could stick a straw in it. I lifted the cap and was trying to pour in the right dose when she came back for her backpack and scared the crap out of me. I was so surprised that my hand jerked, and the entire packet dumped into the bottle. There was no way to get it from her unless I told her I'd been planning to drug her."

My murderer was trying to blame me for my death? This dude was so twisted that if he swallowed a nail, he'd throw up a corkscrew.

If Rez was here, I'd definitely let him eat this goon. Maybe. Probably.

I finally managed to open my eyelids the tiniest sliver. It didn't help. My eyes refused to focus, so all the crack did was cause my head to throb from the bright light.

"How much do you think she drank?" Goon One at least seemed to care about trying to keep me alive.

"I watched her chug the entire bottle down."

"That packet had enough powder to kill a three-hundred-and-fifty-pound man," the nicer goon cursed. The shoulder I'd been thrown over bounced me. "She only weighs a third of that. It's going to kill her for sure!"

I was still stuck on the part where he watched me drink

the whole bottle and hadn't considered stopping me. I wished I could get my hands on him, but my magic was just out of my reach in my semi-paralyzed state.

Goon Two's shrill scream had tears pricking my eyes. Wasn't it enough that he murdered me? Why did he have to torture me, too? I had a hangover from the bad side of Hades, and the least he could do was keep his voice down.

"What is wrong with you?" the less horrible man whisper yelled.

That was how you showed respect for those of us who were about to get their return-to-sender stamp.

"This stupid pig bit me! Look, I'm bleeding!"

"Shut up! Do you want to announce to the whole complex that we participated in this forced meeting?" Goon One snapped. "Stop your whining. That pig isn't big enough to make a decent football."

Albert.

Knowing he was here with me and at these guys' mercy pushed a bit more of the fog from my brain.

"I'm going to turn him into a pigskin if he bites me again," the dickladle snarled.

Albert squealed in pain, and my sluggish heart jerked hard.

"What are you doing?!" Goon One hissed.

"He'll be fine. I just pinched him so he'd think twice before biting me again."

No one threatened my beloved bacon and got away with it. Ignoring the skull-crushing pain ricocheting through my head, I concentrated on my magic.

I called out to it, begging it to come play. It was stupid, since I was in no position to control an onslaught of my magic flooding my body. I was too high to care about the consequences.

I just wanted my murderer to regret all his life choices and realize he done messed up when he messed with me.

My magic was just reaching for me when the men stopped walking.

"Don't tell the boss you gave her too much. Maybe he'll think she is having an allergic reaction," Goon One advised Goon Two.

All right, I didn't like either of them now.

And who was going to keep me from telling? I was absolutely going to be filing a complaint with his boss and HR before I left.

There was a soft whirr as an automatic door slid open.

The men were silent as they strode down a gray concrete corridor and entered another set of glass doors.

"It's about time! Every minute I sit here waiting on you two to skip in here is a missed opportunity."

"Sorry, boss," the men answered together.

Shoes tapped against the concrete, and fingers grabbed my chin to look into my face. The blinding artificial lighting strips caused tears to blur my vision, making it impossible to see the man's face. But I knew his voice from the moment he opened his mouth.

Bartholomew.

CHAPTER NINETEEN
-ARIZONA-

What do you call a dinosaur after a breakup?
TYRANNOSAURUS EX!

When I'd been listening to Hansel and Gretel bicker about their boss, my brain hadn't even processed the part where they'd been ordered to drug me. What had Goon One said when he saw me?

Oh yeah. Bart wanted them to get me high, so he could manipulate me into doing what he wanted.

I should have let Rez eat him. It would have saved us a lot of headaches.

"What's wrong with her?" Bartholomew demanded, his footsteps moving away from me as he took his seat again. "I said I wanted her tipsy and in a good mood. She's barely breathing."

"Maybe she had a reaction to the drug?" Goon Two suggested.

"Hm. I suppose it's possible. Although I believe it is more likely you found a way to screw this up like you screw everything else up." Bart's voice was calm, but vicious.

"Lighten up, Bart. We're family, remember?"

Clearly, all the nuts on that family tree were half-cracked and rotten.

Suli would have cracked up if she'd been in my mind, but my brain was silent of banter and teasing from my bestie, and encouragement and compliments from my shifter mates. The only sound in my skull was my own commentary, and the painful pounding of my headache.

I was always threatening to learn to shield my mind so I'd have privacy, but I'd have given anything to hear their voices at that moment. If I survived this, and Jack wanted it, I'd put my magical energy into creating a mental bridge between him, Rez, and Zon. What if he felt left out?

If I accomplished that, and I got good enough with my magic, I might even try to build a mental chat room so that Suli could talk with not just me, but we'd also have privacy in our original links as well. Right now, the last thing I needed was for the guys to hear the stuff she rambled on about in my brain. They'd just encourage her craziness.

"I'm your boss, don't ever call me by my name in the office!" Bart shouted. There was complete silence, and then he sighed. "Sit her down. Let's see if we can rouse her."

I was dropped into the chair like I was nothing more

than a sack of potatoes. Still unable to control my muscles, my limp body began sliding off the seat.

"Don't let her hit the floor, PJ!" Bartholomew barked.

Goon One, a.k.a. PJ, grabbed the back of my shirt and hauled me upright in the chair again. "Now what, boss?"

"I don't know! You two created this mess. Fix it," Bart demanded.

"Hey now, PJ had nothing to do with her being like this—"

"Shut it, JR!" the other two men shouted.

I really wish they'd stop all the yelling. The pain in my head was beginning to make my stomach churn with rising nausea. Not knowing what to do with me, PJ dropped me unceremoniously onto a small couch.

"Fine, we'll give her an hour to sleep it off. Head out for the job but wait for my signal. And JR? Tie that pig's leash to the table chair or something. I don't want him crapping all over my office. Filthy animal."

"Yes, boss." Their heavy footsteps faded, and the whirr of the door signaled they'd left.

It was quiet for so long that I thought Bart must have gone with them. I was unable to turn my head, so I couldn't be sure though. So, when Bartholomew appeared inches above my face, it gave me the jump scare of my life.

Although, by definition, it wasn't a jump scare since I was unable to do any jumping. All I managed was the slightest widening of my eyes.

"Ah, so you are at least somewhat awake in that stubborn little head of yours. Perfect. I need you to answer three questions before I can leave you."

He wanted me to answer him? I could barely breathe, let alone speak.

"Will you sign an exclusive partnership agreement with my company? I know you are the head of Dinovation. I've been in business long enough to recognize another leader—even one as lacking as you. You will be paid handsomely for half ownership of Dinovation. We will share 50/50 rights to the prototypes, and have equal decision-making power for the future of the company. Close your eyes for yes, blink twice for no."

Without hesitation, I fluttered my lashes.

"I thought you might say that. Money doesn't seem to matter as much to you. But see, it does to the rest of the world, and you could really screw up the robotic market if you undersell or start giving away info. I can't have that. Not after my company has spent years developing our own line of hyper-realistic robotics."

I stared at him, pushing as much hate as I could into my gaze.

"Now for my second question. Will you sign over half the company and its assets in exchange for me not burning the warehouse with your prototypes in it to the ground?"

My eyes widened and the bile churning in my stomach filled my throat, threatening to choke me.

"My company is very successful, but your robotics have an edge that my team hasn't achieved yet. I've invested everything into building this business, and I will lose it all if you beat me to market. If I have to lose everything, then you will too."

I frantically searched his face, looking for any sign he was bluffing, but he was dead serious. I reached for my magic, but it was just out of my reach. I was helpless to save the ones I loved more than anything on Earth.

Bart lifted the phone to his mouth. "Is the team in place?"

"Absolutely, boss. That Oliver guy is bringing the dinos to the warehouse now," PJ answered.

"Good. And the feed?"

There was some muffled chatter on the other end of the line, then PJ spoke. "JR said it's live now. Does that mean we have your go ahead, boss?"

Bart pulled the phone away from his mouth. "I'll give you one more chance to accept my second offer and save your beloved toys. Will you partner with my company? Yes or no? I won't ask again, princess."

Tears leaked from my eyes. Surely my men would see the trap a mile away.

Maybe I could agree and then report Bartholomew.

"Don't go there. I can see the calculating look in your eye. If you agree to the contract, I have layers of security built into it. I created the garden proposal to keep you here long enough to create an incredibly detailed paper trail that makes you and Jack Oliver look like pretty nasty people. Oh, and we would get married. It would be hard to prove you were under duress when you'd be living a fairytale. Poor museum cleaner marries millionaire. Then, if you try to turn me in for shady dealings, it wouldn't look so hot for you, especially without any type of proof. Give me your final answer."

I had to trust my men to protect themselves, because there was no way I could take the vows to love this man. Not after I'd experienced the true love of a fated mate.

"Let me help you decide." Bart picked up a remote and clicked the buttons.

Satisfied, he sat the remote down and angled my head to the side so that I was staring straight at a large screen TV.

A live stream of the warehouse was playing, and I watched in horror as Jack led the shifters inside, keeping up the pretense that they were animatronics.

Bart squatted next to the couch, so our faces were level.

"Tick tock. What's it going to be? Yes, or no?"

If I agreed, he would figure out the 'robotics' were real dinos. Their safety would be jeopardized, and Bart would never let them live a life of freedom. We'd lose everything, and I would have betrayed my mates by promising my body and heart to someone else.

If I said no, they might not get out in time. They could die, and it would be my fault. But I knew what they would want me to do, and I needed to trust their abilities.

Tears leaked from my eyes as I fluttered my eyelashes again.

Bart lifted his phone to his mouth. "Go."

No sooner had he finished speaking, than several men rushed forward and barricaded the doors with thick steel beams.

And then they set the building on fire.

Bart stared at my face as I watched my entire world burn to the ground. I couldn't even sob because my body refused to respond to my commands.

"It didn't have to be this way." Bart wiped a tear from my cheek. "Such a stubborn, selfish woman. And look what it got you? Oh! And sweetheart, I've set this little fiasco up to look like it was a turf war. If you go to the cops, I have more evidence I've planted to convince the police this was all orchestrated by you. Walk away, and keep your pretty little mouth shut."

Standing, he strolled from the room with a bounce in his step and whistling a jaunty tune.

He thought he was so smart, planning every little detail.

But if my mates were gone, I'd have nothing left in this world to lose.

He will have wished he'd killed me too, because I would make his misery my sole purpose for however long I survived.

WHEN THE FIRE had finally died out, the goons returned and moved a subdued Albert and me to a tiny, windowless space.

"Did you hear the fire department has already found two bodies in the burned remains of the warehouse?"

I didn't know a heart could make an audible sound as it broke… until I heard mine.

They'd already found two bodies. Even if the other two escaped, I'd lost two of the people I loved more than life.

"PJ, that makes no sense. We checked the building for other people when we went through looking for their research data right before they returned from the museum. The only human was the detective." JR looked worried. "You think we overlooked someone? This ain't good, PJ."

They laid me on another small couch and tossed Albert onto the slick floor, where his small body rolled several times before coming to a stop.

I wanted to scream or blast them with magic, but the drug was still moving sluggishly through my veins. It probably would have killed me if I had been fully human, and I suspected it was my magic that was keeping me alive until the drug moved through my system.

Their deaths would not be quick.

"Okay, missy. This is part of the parking garage for the office complex. Even if you survive the drugs and can start screaming, no one can hear you. Bart is going to let you go, so I suggest you just be a good guest and rest until he gives us the all-clear to release you." PJ was making it sound like they were just watching out for me. What a load of dung.

The only reason Bart was letting me live was because he wanted me to suffer for telling him no. He wanted me to wake up every day and know what I lost because I wouldn't bow to his demands. He wanted me to know he'd won.

But he hadn't. His day was coming.

When the goons shut the door to the small room, there was an audible click as they locked me inside. Bart's newest toy until he got bored of taunting me.

Albert made his way to the sofa, and thanks to a footstool, he managed to get up on the couch with me. Pushing his cool, wet nose under my elbow, he scooted forward until my limp arm lay over him.

Fresh tears streaked down my face, and unable to deal with everything going on, I closed my eyes and prayed for sleep to take me away from this nightmare.

CHAPTER TWENTY
-ARIZONA-

What do you call a raptor who can't accept defeat?
A SAUR LOSER.

I was shaken from my dream when an explosion rocked the foundation of the building. Plaster fell from the ceiling, and the walls groaned as they began buckling. For a split second, I had a flashback to that night in the museum when Rez and Zon had awakened.

A section of the wall behind the couch started crumbling, sending chunks of concrete tumbling onto the couch. With the wall no longer bearing weight thanks to the unstable foundation, the ceiling sagged, and thick cracks began to spread.

From outside, came the intermittent staccato pop-pop-pop of gunfire, tires screeched, and male voices shouted curses over the eardrum-rattling explosions.

Albert shoved his nose against my face. He licked and

squealed, urging me to move my butt. Oh right! I was about to be buried beneath the concrete parking garage.

My brain sent the order telling my legs to move, but nothing happened. Over and over, I tried to get my legs to respond, even as increasingly larger pieces of the wall and ceiling rained down on me.

"Go." With effort, I managed to croak out the single word.

I desperately hoped my beloved pig would understand I wanted him to find a safe corner to hide in.

Albert ignored my command, and continued to shove at my limp body. He was frantic in his efforts to push me from the couch, and away from the crumbling wall.

Turning my attention to my arms, I tried to move them and was relieved when I got a finger to twitch in response. My muscle control was returning… and if it managed to come back fast enough, I might be able to avoid being flattened under the weight of the concrete.

Surviving, meant I would be able to hunt Bart down.

Focusing my foggy brain wasn't easy, but after several more tries, one arm slid across the sofa cushion. It took a few more attempts before my second arm began to move as well. Moving with the speed of a turtle, I finally managed to pull the dead weight of my body from the couch.

Once I was on the floor, I used my arms to move my torso enough that I could inspect the room's four walls. All four showed obvious signs of stress, but the one that was going to fall first was the one behind the sofa.

Gathering what energy I could, with painstaking effort I

army crawled away from the sofa. If I was lucky, maybe I wouldn't be buried beneath it when it collapsed. A rumbling aftershock shook the ground.

Had the apocalypse started while I was unconscious? My brain was struggling to make sense of anything that had happened since I'd left the museum.

The memory of the warehouse burning to the ground sent fresh tears streaming down my cheeks. I wanted to curl in a ball and give up. But my heart didn't want to accept that my family was truly gone. And if they were still alive, I needed to fight to survive.

Albert walked beside me, matching my pace and nudging me when my trembling arms gave out. My eyes burned from the sweat dripping into them as I strained my weak muscles to move one slow inch at a time.

We gave it a good try, but in the end, our efforts simply didn't matter.

Another explosion hit the building, and the wall couldn't handle the strain and collapsed into the small room. Without the wall supporting any of its weight, the entire ceiling caved in as well.

The world seemed to move in slow motion as pieces of concrete began to fall. For a brief moment, I was able to see parts of the parking garage overhead. Light glinted on a chrome bumper as a car began to roll into the hole being created in the weakened ceiling.

We were about to be flattened, and unable to flee and Albert refusing to leave my side, I did the only thing I could. Grabbing Albert, I tucked him under me. Maybe if my body took the brunt of the impact, he might survive. Then I called to my distant magic, begging it to protect him.

Light poured into the room as the ceiling and walls of the entire concrete structure above began to collapse. And then we were plunged into darkness as we were buried beneath it.

MY RETURN to consciousness was a brutal experience. Excruciating pain was trying to tear my body apart, and I opened my mouth to scream, but nothing came out.

Okay, I really had died this time, and I'd landed in Dante's hell. That was the only logical explanation for the flicking flames dotting the darkness surrounding me, the burning rubber and oil that coated my tongue and lungs with each breath I forced in. Not to mention the white-hot agony scorching through every cell in my body.

"Arizona. You're not in hell. You're on Earth and you're in a bad situation." The male voice was angelic, and completely unfamiliar.

Groaning in pain, I twisted my head around to see who the voice belonged to, only to find a stranger. A stranger who was on his knees, his body straddling mine as he used his body to protect me. He was the only thing keeping me from being flattened.

Wait. Hadn't the man spoken my name? That meant he knew me. Maybe we'd met and I'd forgotten him? I studied his face as best I could in the dim light.

The man's body was lean, but still muscular. He didn't appear to be older than thirty, yet his hair was carbon gray. Although I couldn't say if it was from the coat of concrete dust that covered everything, or if that was his true hair color. Beads of sweat trickled down his face, leaving wet streaks through the grime.

I didn't recognize him. Except. His eyes?

There was something familiar about them. Or maybe I was simply hallucinating due to the drugs still in my bloodstream, and the searing agony that made it hard to even breathe?

I pressed my shaking fingers to my temple. It was hard to think clearly when I was being stabbed through the skull. How had the man even gotten down here? Had he been in the parking garage above me and fallen through? His muscles trembled violently, and he hissed.

"Are you hurt?" I tried to roll my body over so I could check on him, and immediately wished I hadn't when a tsunami of agony tore through me.

"Stop trying to move!" the stranger growled. "You're pinned under several pieces of concrete. I'd love to free you, but a large piece of the concrete and steel support column is currently trying to crush us. I'm trying to stop that from happening, but I need your help." His voice shook as the strain grew harder to handle.

"How can I help you? I can't even help myself or—" A

sob caught in my throat and my heart froze in terror as I realized I hadn't felt Albert squirming under me.

Where was he? Maybe he'd managed to escape?

"Albert!" I screamed, voice breaking.

I couldn't lose him too.

"Right here."

I shifted my upper body the best I could, staring up at the man arched over me.

"You don't understand!" I sobbed. "Albert is my pig. Did you see him escape? He has to be okay!"

"I am *your* Albert," the man growled, his muscles rippling as he strained against the concrete column. "Don't look so shocked, Arizona. We both know you'd already guessed I was more than just your pet pig."

This was a dream—something my mind created to make sense of what was happening around my unconscious body. Yes, that was it. I'd hit my head and ended up in some weird version of Oz.

"This is real, but we're running out of time."

"You're a shifter?" If this wasn't a dream, how could he be Albert?

"Not exactly, but that is a long story and not one I prefer to tell while we are at risk of being squashed." He tried to laugh, but his breathing was ragged.

"It wasn't supposed to happen like this, and not this soon." His pale blue eyes begged me to believe him. "I wanted our first meeting in this form to be different. But neither of us can change what has already been done."

"How can I help you?" I whispered, honestly struggling to process anything that was happening.

"Ari, I need your magic. You have to send magic into me like you did with Rez when you forced his shift."

I shook my head. "I can't reach my magic. There's a disconnect, and it's out of my reach."

A shiver traveled the length of my body. Why was it so cold? I stiffened when another realization smacked me in the face. The pain was gone. My body was no longer in agony. I felt nothing.

"Look at me!" Albert ordered, and my eyes locked with his. "You are dying, Ari. Your legs sustained severe injuries. I blocked most of the blows to your torso and head, but you have internal bleeding. If I don't heal you, you will die."

"Then why are you still here? If I'm already dying, then leave me and save yourself!" I growled.

"I'm here because you're mine." His eyes glowed, silver swirling within the blue of his irises. "I can save you, but you have to be willing to fight to survive."

My jaw dropped.

If he was telling the truth about being Albert, then the adorable pet pig I delighted in dressing up in ridiculous outfits just told me I was his.

What did he mean when he said I was his?

"Touch me," the stranger growled, sweat dripping from his hair and body. "I'd touch you, but my hands are full at the moment."

On autopilot, I reached out, but stopped before making contact with his skin.

"I won't bite—fine, I sometimes bite—but you're in no danger of being bitten right now. Press your fingers to my skin," he repeated.

The moment my palm touched his skin, electricity sizzled through my body. Yanking my hand away like I'd been burned, I stared at him, my brain not able to process what had just happened.

"You're my mate." His eyes glittered. "And I'm yours."

My mouth opened and closed, but nothing came out. What could I say?

"I've waited so long to say those words to you… to feel the spark when my fated mate touched my skin." When I said nothing, he continued, "How do you think I was able to speak in your mind today when I told you to look down? It was the mate bond creating a link between us as your magic has grown."

"That was you? I thought it was Jack." My world had been turned upside down and shaken. Nothing made sense.

"Arizona. You felt it when you touched my skin. You know it's the truth." He was almost desperate to have me acknowledge it.

"Yes," I whispered. "I felt it."

I'd felt the pull of the fated mate spark, and thanks to Tsufnu, I had the ability to sense a perfect match.

Albert was both… and that terrified me.

But if he'd known all this time, why had he hidden it from me?

"I guessed this might happen when you first found out. I will explain things, but this is not the time. Call your magic, Ari. Hurry!" he grunted, closing his eyes to focus on keeping the column from falling on us.

Closing my eyes, I reached for my magic, begging it to help. Slowly, as though moving through molasses, it tried to answer my call.

"You've got to do this faster," Albert hissed between clenched teeth. "Send the magic to me, and then reach out to Rez and guide him to where we're buried. He knows you're close by, but he's struggling to locate you."

"Rez is alive?" I whispered, hope blossoming in my chest.

"I thought you knew! Can't you hear his roars? All three dinosaurs are here searching for you. I've heard Jack calling your name too."

They were all alive.

My family was alive.

My eyes flashed to meet Albert's gaze.

All of them.

There was a lot to unpack between us, but he'd been my family before the others had joined us. We'd have to see what happened in the future, but none of that mattered at the moment. He was alive, and I was thankful for that.

"Let's get out of here. I want to go home." Closing my eyes, I centered myself and focused like I'd done the night I'd forced Rez to shift to his human form.

Grabbing hold of my magic, I pulled it from its drug-induced stupor. The instant it was free, my magic roared to life, ready to do whatever it took to get us out of here alive.

It had been a sucky day, and it was time to burn off

steam.

Before I released my magic, I found the link I shared with Rez and Zon. It was weak, thanks to the drug's lingering effects on my brain, but it was undamaged.

Rez? Zon?

From somewhere outside the rubble, I could hear the dinos' bellows of relief when they heard my voice.

You're alive! We could sense your body, but we didn't know if you were alive. When the mental link was cut off, and we couldn't reach you, we thought… Rez trailed off, not wanting to finish the thought.

I was drugged, and shut down everything in my body, including my connections with you three. Rez, I need you to come get Albert and me out. We're trapped under the parking garage, and a stone column is about to crush us.

We're coming, Ari. Zon's voice was rough with emotion.

Hang in there, bestie! Suli laughed, and it was filled with relief and joy that they'd found us in time. *This was a life sentence, and you just started doing your time. You're stuck with me.*

I'm going to have to focus on a situation we have going on down here. I tried to be vague, not wanting them to find out I was alive, and then immediately find out I was dying. *I'm going to send up a blast of magic. Watch for it. Maybe it will help you find us quicker.*

We're watching. Go! Zon rumbled.

I began spinning my magic into a tight ball, and with a surge of energy, I sent it blasting up above our heads.

"Shield your eyes!" Albert yelled, as concrete dust and

shards of steel rained down on us.

My tyrannosaurus mate bellowed directly above our heads, letting us know he was there. The next thing I heard was screeching metal as Rez began tossing cars away so he could get to us.

Albert growled, fighting the concrete. "I need you to focus, Arizona. I have to stop your bleeding and I need to be charged up to do it. Flatten your hands against my stomach and release the magic into me. My body is made to handle your magic, so don't worry about hurting me. Just hurry!"

That raised so many questions, but he was right. They'd have to wait.

Twisting my upper body the best I could, I pressed my hands lightly to Albert's stomach.

"Ari, I know this is weird. But for this to work, I need you to trust me. Now blast me like you mean it!"

And so, I did. I harnessed the anger I felt at Bartholomew for what he'd done, my anger over how JR had treated my pig, and finally, I drew on the fresh hurt and betrayal I felt at Albert being able to shift, but never telling me. All those nights I needed a shoulder to cry on...

I was there.

His voice was in my head.

Ari, when you need to be soothed, you enjoy stroking my ears to ease your stress.

I've been siphoning magic off you since the day you brought me home, making sure you didn't hurt yourself before the time was right and you had more support to protect you and teach you.

I have been there. Just not in a human form.

There were rules that had to be followed, and things that had to happen for me to be able to reveal myself to you.

"You were supposed to be my friend, and you lied!" I screamed, sending every bit of magic I could muster surging into him.

Albert's silvery-blue eyes shifted to pink. The exact same hue as my magic.

The instant his irises changed; the strain vanished from his face. With Herculean ease, he shoved the column away from us and within seconds, he'd moved the large pieces of concrete that pinned my legs.

Leaning over me, Albert whispered, "Whether you believe it right now or not, I am your friend in every form I take. I belong to you. It isn't my fault that I couldn't reveal myself to you, and I never lied to you. I will never lie to you."

His hand pressed to my lower back, and immediately my magic began flowing back in to me. It was my magic… but also slightly different. Like a flood, it rushed through my body, searching for every injury.

Albert spoke again, his voice shaking with sorrow. "I'm not a shifter, nor am I Vazi. When things are not so life-or-death, I want to tell you everything." He reached to brush his knuckles across my face, but stopped himself.

The longing in his eyes was my undoing, and I caved… a little.

"Go ahead."

His knuckles brushed my skin, and he sucked in a harsh

breath. "I've wanted to do that every time I've had to watch you cry. There was nothing I wanted more than to hold you."

"Then why didn't you?"

"Because it was either be your pet until the time was right and I could reveal myself, or never have a chance with you at all." His eyes fell away from mine, and he cleared his throat.

"Give me time," I whispered.

Albert's eyes met mine again, letting me see the raw love and pain in their depths. "I'd give you forever if you asked it of me."

My nerve endings tingled as little by little the feeling began to return to my limbs. I didn't understand how, but Albert had managed to guide my magic, healing my broken body and cleansing the rest of the drug from my system.

When he finished, he pulled his hand from my back. "Ari, I'm going to return to the pig form. Take as long as you need, but when you are ready, send your magic into me, and I will be able to take this form again and tell you everything. It's important for you to understand I can't change forms without a surge of your magic to power it."

I didn't want to admit it to him, but I was relieved by his offer. Too much had happened in the last twenty-four hours, and I needed time to rest and sort through it.

A minute later, when Rez pulled away the last piece of concrete blocking us in, I was healed, and a familiar tiny pig sat by my feet.

It was time to go home.

CHAPTER TWENTY-ONE
-ARIZONA-

What do you call a triceratops that won't stop talking?
A DINO-BORE.

Stepping from the shower, I dried off quickly and pulled one of Jack's T-shirts over my head. I could have grabbed a pair of my pajamas, but I preferred wearing one of my guys' shirts to sleep in.

Although, most nights, anything I put on ended up being tossed to the floor.

What can I say? Sharing a bed with my three gorgeous mates made it really hard to keep my hands to myself. Not that they were complaining.

Heading into the bedroom, I paused in the doorway and took a moment to just drink in the sight in front of me. When we'd gotten back to Jack's—I mean, *our*—home three days before, I'd been delighted when Jack revealed that he'd had a custom bed made for us.

It took up most of the room, but it allowed us to share a bed without feeling crowded. I loved being cuddled and squished between my men, but while the guys liked snuggling with me, they didn't feel the same about accidentally snuggling up to each other while asleep.

Rez and Zon were both shirtless, and had their backs propped up on the bed's headboard. There was a gap exactly my size between them. Jack lay horizontally across the foot of the bed, his arms propped behind his head.

Contentedness warmed my body from head to toes. My life was just about perfect.

Turning his head, Jack caught me staring and winked. "Are you going to come to bed, Firefly? Or do you just want to stand there and admire our collective sexiness for the rest of the night?"

Laughing, I ran across the floor and threw myself onto the bed.

The moment my body hit the puffy mattress, Rez shifted to lie beside me. His arm hooked over my waist, pulling me against his body.

Rez playfully nipped my neck. "I missed you."

"I was only in the shower for fifteen minutes." Unable to resist, I caught his face between my hands and kissed him, hoping he would feel how much I loved him since I couldn't seem to find the words.

Rez deepened the kiss, turning me on in a way only my mates could, and it took all my will-power to pull away. For the last three days, I'd done nothing but sleep, eat, and find comfort—and pleasure—in my mates' arms.

I hadn't wanted to even think about what we'd just gone through. It was too raw, too fresh. But my heart was feeling less raw, and there were questions I needed the answers to.

I blew out a long breath. "How did you all survive the fire? And how did you know where I was?"

Jack rolled onto his side, propping himself up on one hand. "Are you sure you're ready to talk about this?"

My men had respected my request to just enjoy our time together for a few days before we hashed out the events of that day.

At my nod, Jack sat up and pulled my feet onto his lap. "Then let's do this. After I put you in the rideshare, we worked until closing as planned. When we were about to leave, I called my buddy at the police station to get an update on John Smith. Turns out, John's fingerprints matched the fingerprints found in a recent string of burglaries."

"Wow! I never would have expected that! He sucked at being sneaky. I'm finding it hard to imagine he was a professional thief." I guess you never knew about people.

"I have to admit it surprised me, too." Jack's fingers massaged my feet as he continued. "When John realized he'd been busted, he decided he needed to do whatever he could to get a lighter sentence. He started singing like a bird about every crime he'd ever heard about, and he'd heard through the grapevine that some guys working for

Burkhardt were asking around for some help for a job going down that afternoon."

Blood pounded in my ears. "The attack on the warehouse?"

Jack nodded. "With the cops listening in, John called a few friends and found one who'd agreed to take the job. That guy was happy to tell John all about it, providing the details the cops needed to get a team together."

"I can't believe how fast they worked on this. The friend of yours must really like you." I twisted my shirt between my fingers, knowing where the story was going and feeling the panic that hit me every time the memories of the fire played in my mind.

Breathe, Arizona. They are alive. We are all safe. How many times had I repeated those words to myself since we'd arrived home? Too many.

"He's a good guy, but the entire force moved fast because this was the break they had been waiting on. Bartholomew Burkhardt had been on their radar for a long time. They'd suspected he was using less than legal methods to convince competitors to partner with him, but he was slick. Every time they started following a lead, Bartholomew would lay down evidence that hurt the credibility of their witnesses."

I hadn't realized I was chewing my thumbnail until Rez gently caught my hand and laced his fingers through mine. "Ari, are you sure you want to do this? It can wait."

"No. It's like ripping the Band-Aid off. Let's get it over with so I can move forward. Hey, where is Suli?" The house was awfully quiet, and I hadn't seen her since we'd shared lunch on the porch swing.

Zon snickered. "She discovered what binge-watching means. We saw her grab a sandwich for dinner and then rush back to her room for the next episode."

"Uh oh. What show and how many seasons are we talking about?" I knew I was delaying because I didn't want to hear about the warehouse attack, but I couldn't help it.

"Nineteen," Jack answered. "She's watching Grey's Anatomy."

"That will take her—"

Approximately 272 hours and 33 minutes for me to get caught up to season 19, Suli answered in my mind.

Are you reading my thoughts again? I pretended to sound grouchy, but truthfully, I was happy to hear her.

I'd never felt as alone as I did when the drug took away the link between the shifters and me. It taught me I didn't want silence in my mind.

Nooo. I was minding my own business, enjoying my show when I sensed your anxiety, and like the good bestie I am, I decided to check-in. If you're good, I'm going to tune you out and go back to my show.

I could practically feel the force of Suli's eyeroll. The sarcasm was strong with that one. *I'm fine. Just need to work through these pesky emotions. Let me know when you make it to season 12. I got busy and stopped watching, so we could binge the rest of the series together.*

Will do! And Ari? If you need me, just let me know. Now shut up, it's coming back on!

I hadn't wanted to awaken another 'gift' from my grandmother, but I had to admit, Suli added something to my life I hadn't even realized I'd been missing. Hopefully, I could do the same for her.

"Okay, keep going." I crossed my arms over my chest, determined to push through.

Jack didn't argue and picked up right where he had left off. "I was asked to be part of the take-down operation. Right before we left the museum to head for the warehouse, we realized something was really wrong. It was confirmed when my friend called to let me know they had a new tip from John about a female matching your description being drugged and taken."

Rez's chest vibrated beneath my ear as he whispered a series of clicks and trills into my hair. "Jack found your backpack and the water bottle. There was just enough left in the bottle for us to see there was residue. It took all my control not to rampage through the city until I found you. I would have done it, if we hadn't already had a plan in place that would hopefully lead us to where Bartholomew might have you. Plus, it would give the cops the evidence they needed to get him off the streets… and away from you."

When Rez didn't say anything more, Jack spoke. "We headed back to the museum just like we had planned. We entered the building, and it was almost immediately set on fire. PJ made the call to his boss to confirm the job was done, and then the thugs all scrambled to get out of there."

"But they weren't fast enough. That's when the SWAT team lying in wait leaped into action. John's friend talked about how the job had to be done just right because it was being watched live by their boss. So the cops were prepared. Their tech team hacked the video feed, creating a feedback loop of the last sixty seconds of footage that had been recorded of the burning warehouse."

With the drugs immobilizing me, I hadn't been able to turn away that video and the footage was burned into my brain.

My heart thudded against my ribcage, and I fought my growing anxiety.

"Deep breaths, my queen." Rez held me against his chest.

After a few minutes of listening to the steady thump of Rez's heart, I had pulled myself together—as much as I could, anyway. "Keep going, Jack. Please."

Jack hesitated, and I thought he was going to argue, but then he continued where we'd left off. "The loop made it appear the video feed was still live to whoever was watching it, which bought the SWAT team the time they needed to open the back of the warehouse to get the dinos and myself out. They were also able to apprehend all the criminals who had participated. Only PJ and JR were allowed to leave, because the cops hoped to trail them back to wherever Bartholomew was hiding. And hopefully where he had you. Once that was finished, the video began showing the livestream of the burning warehouse."

I sat up, my brow creasing. "But the newscaster said they'd found two bodies. Whose bodies were they?"

Jack shook his head. "There were no bodies. The

reporter had been coached on what to say. She said two, because the cops thought it might make Bartholomew nervous to know his men hadn't done the job right. We were all willing to do anything if it might make him clumsy or cause him to make a mistake."

The warehouse had truly burned to the ground, but no one had died. There was just one more thing I needed to know…

"What the heck happened at Bartholomew's office building and the parking garage? It was in ruins when we left!"

"Rezkac happened." Zon punched the T-Rex shifter playfully.

"So Rez is the one who brought down the parking garage on top of me?"

The men looked horrified.

"No! Of course not!" Rez thundered. "We had no idea there were small offices beneath the garage, but it was Bartholomew who brought the building down."

"What? Why would he destroy his office and garage?" I rubbed at my aching temples.

"He didn't destroy his offices. I did that." Rez puffed his chest up. "He shouldn't have stolen my mate, and he shouldn't have ordered his security to fire at my family. I stopped them, and he lost his office in the process."

"As for the parking garage," Jack interjected, "my friend tells me that they've found what was left of a storage room filled with falsified evidence that he had created. They'd also recovered some old hard drives that have yielded more clues in tracing his crooked business dealings. The cops believe he tried to destroy the storage room, but in his haste, he made a mistake and set a larger charge than he needed."

"Yeah. The explosions damaged several key support structures within the garage, and the collapse of the office building further shook the foundation. I've never experienced terror like I felt when we finally sensed you and realized you were buried beneath the rubble." Zon lifted my hand to his mouth and kissed it.

I smiled at each of my mates in turn. "But you guys found me. Saved me."

Just like Albert had saved me. First by keeping me from being crushed to death, and then by healing me.

"Where's Bart now?" This had been weighing on my mind since I'd been pulled from the dark garage. I'd wanted to know if he was out there and might come for me, but I'd been too afraid to ask.

"He's in jail, and he is going to stay there a long time— probably the rest of his lifetime and several more." Jack squeezed my foot gently. "He won't ever get to touch you again. He is truly out of our lives."

I hoped he was right.

"One more thing." I focused on Jack. "Do the cops really believe the dinosaurs who helped them take down Bartholomew and his security guards are robotics? Their movements were far too lifelike, and there was no way you kept up the pretense of using the remote on them during the heat of the firefight."

Jack huffed a soft laugh. "To be honest, they don't know what to think. They appreciated our help and didn't want to deal with the headache of questioning us. If people found out they'd even entertained the idea that we had live dinosaurs, it would be assumed that they were crazy or high. I don't think we need to worry."

Several long minutes passed as I stared unseeing at the comforter. I had my answers and now I could forget about Bartholomew and focus on life with my mates. It was time for the next chapter.

Jack smacked his head. "Oh! Before I forget. Teresa called and left a message for you while you were showering."

"Really?" I wished I'd had the chance to say bye to her before Zon teleported us home.

"She sounded pretty upset over introducing you to Bart. I think she feels like somehow it is her fault. She wanted us to know that she'd spoken to a friend of hers in Utah, who's invited us up to enjoy a little getaway in a month. They've been working a dig site up there and thought we'd love a behind-the-scenes look." Jack smiled, excitement dancing in his eyes. "I have to admit. It sounds pretty cool!"

"I don't know, guys. Maybe we should stick around here for a while." The trip sounded fun, but I was not sure I ever wanted to leave the safety of these four walls again.

"Utah. That name is familiar. I have been studying modern maps to locate some of the items we wish to collect. I believe Utah is one of the places we need to go." Rez rubbed his jawline. "This could be perfect timing."

"I think it could be fun. We need a vacation," Zon agreed.

All three men stared at me, their faces reminding me of begging puppies.

"Ugh! I can't say no to you guys!" I threw up my hands in defeat. "No promises, but I'll talk to Teresa tomorrow and get more information. Then we can decide."

The guys practically smothered me in kisses, and I knew I wouldn't be able to say no if they really wanted to go.

From the corner of my eye, I caught sight of Albert sitting in the doorway.

While I had told the guys an abbreviated version of what happened after Jack put me in the car, no one knew about Albert. Or what he'd become while we'd been buried beneath the rubble.

I'd known the shifters would likely sift through my thoughts and find the memories, but I'd wanted to keep that piece of info to myself for a bit.

It had taken an incredible amount of magic, but I'd been able to create a wall around the memories of those minutes I'd been trapped in. All three shifters likely knew I was keeping something from them, but they were giving me space.

I would make sure everyone knew the truth, but I needed time to sort out my own thoughts first. And at some point, I needed to talk to Albert.

Rez and Zon stiffened at Albert's sudden appearance, but Jack grinned. "The little guy must be feeling better!"

After Zon had teleported us all home, Albert had been

giving me space. Everyone had noticed that the pig barely left his plush dog bed, other than to drink water and eat a few bites of food.

Jack had tried to take him to the vet this morning, and I'd barely managed to talk him out of it. I'd taken Albert to the vet for yearly checkups, but I hadn't known he wasn't really a pig.

I cringed thinking of what each of those visits had entailed. On the bright side, I hadn't gotten him neutered yet. Which meant he should be thanking me that he'd only gotten a thermometer up the butt, right?

Albert laid down on the edge of the bedroom carpet, making sure I knew he was there for me, but not pushing me for things to go back to how they'd been before.

I'd accused Albert of not being there for me when I was alone, and he'd said he had always been there for me. He was right.

Because in this moment when my heart was raw from painful memories, I missed his reassuring presence.

"Albert?" I whispered.

He sat up, tilting his head and waiting.

"Come here."

Ever thoughtful, Jack had a small ramp built and placed it at the foot of the bed, allowing Albert to trot up it and onto the mattress. Zon scooted to the side to give the little ham more room. He still wasn't comfortable around Albert, but was willing to deal with it for my sake.

Albert sat down next to me, letting me again take the

lead in our first real interaction since his secret had been revealed.

Lifting him into my arms, I breathed in the familiar scent of the oatmeal shampoo I washed him in.

Not wanting anyone else to overhear, I whispered next to his ear, "I'm still upset with you. But I miss my friend."

I hoped he understood I was acknowledging I'd been wrong to say he wasn't my friend. My heart sank when Albert wiggled out of my arms, ran down the ramp, and disappeared down the hallway. I hadn't meant to hurt him.

Before I could burst into tears, he darted back through the doorway and up onto the bed. Hopping onto my lap, he dropped the item he'd gone to retrieve.

His favorite stuffed toy.

He nosed the plush pig on my lap.

How many times had he done this when I was sad in the past? I couldn't even count. Each time he'd brought me his toy, it was as though he understood I was hurting and wanted to make me happy by giving me his favorite thing.

After seeing him in a human male body, I knew he didn't really have an attachment to the toy. But it had been one of the only ways he had to show me how much he cared, without being able to speak.

I'd asked for him to be the pet pig I loved until I was ready to talk. And by giving me the stuffed toy, just as he'd done to make me smile in the past, he was letting me know he understood. He was willing to let me pretend.

My eyes blurred with unshed tears, and I tucked him in my arms. Rubbing my cheek against his velvety ear, I felt the familiar calm that always poured through me in his presence.

Settling down under the covers, surrounded by the ones I loved the most, the rest of my worry and fear faded away. Tomorrow was a new day, and I was both excited and slightly terrified to see what it would bring.

CHAPTER TWENTY-TWO
-ALBERT-

How did the dinosaur feel after he was reassembled at the museum, and then woke up?
PUZZLED.

I t shouldn't be possible for someone to be in both heaven and hell at the same time. But yet here I was, doing the impossible.

Arizona had fallen asleep, her arm still clutching me tight, and her soft cheek brushing against the top of my head. Being close to her in any form was special, but I was desperate to experience what it would be like when I could hold her as a man.

I wanted to kiss away her tears, instead of being forced to use a silly toy to show I understood she was hurting and wanted to make her happy. Since the day she brought me home, it had been hard to be around my perfect mate—my entire universe—but stuck in a tiny pig's body and unable to tell her.

I'd gotten a tiny taste of what it was like to be around her as a man when I'd healed her, my skin touching hers. Then she'd given me permission to touch her cheek.

I hadn't been ready for the reaction my body would have, or the torrent of churning emotions just that lightest of touches had released inside me.

The memory of her touch on my stomach had been branded into my very soul. I'd waited so long to feel the magic crackle and race between us—the physical sign we were meant for each other.

Tonight, Arizona made it clear she wanted to pretend, at least for a bit, that I'd never changed forms. That I was just an unusually smart, but definitely not magical, pig.

I could feel her pain. She was hurt, and felt betrayed that I'd hidden myself from her. What she didn't yet understand was that my ability to change forms was entirely in her hands.

I had no choice in the matter.

When the building had collapsed, and Arizona had used that last blast of magic to protect me, the drugs had caused her to miscalculate. Instead of a protection dome like she'd intended to place over me, she sent the full force of her magic into me.

It complicated things, but I would forever be grateful. Because had I been stuck as the pig, I would never have been able to save her. But as a man who was charged up on her magic, I'd been able to stop the worst of it, and then heal her injuries.

One day, I prayed I would finally be given my chance. If I had to spend the rest of my life as a pig just to be around her, I would do it without question.

But I longed to have her love me, the being inside the piglet's peachy body. I wanted a chance at having her fall in love with me as she'd done with her three mates.

Arizona wasn't ready to talk to me. She might not be ready for a very long time. That was fine. She could take as long as she needed. I'd been waiting to be with Arizona for a very long time. And I'd still be here waiting at the end of time, because she was the only thing I'd ever wanted.

ABOUT SEDONA ASHE

Sedona Ashe doesn't reserve her sarcasm for her books; her poor husband can tell you that her wit, humor, and snarky attitude are just part of her daily life. While she loves writing paranormal shifter reverse harem novels, she's a sucker for true love, twisted situations, and wacky humor.

Sedona lives in a small town at the base of the Great Smoky Mountains in Tennessee. She and her husband share their home with their three children, adorable pup, five cats, an arctic fox, chickens, several crazy turkeys, two chubby frogs, an emu with happy feet, and over a hundred reptiles. When she isn't working, she enjoys getting away from the computer to hike, free dive, travel, study languages, and capture places and animals in her photography. She has a crazy goal of writing a million words in a year, and spending six months exploring Indonesia.

You can find more information about the author and her books here:

www.authorsedonaashe.com

www.instagram.com/sedonaashe

www.facebook.com/sedonaashe

www.ingramcontent.com/pod-product-compliance
Lightning Source LLC
Chambersburg PA
CBHW030138180626
46812CB00002B/746